LIONS · TRACKS

Now Then, Al

Sixteen year old Alan leaves school with no qualifications and no job to go to. Unemployment in his town is high but his parents don't understand why he can't find a job. After a bad row Alan takes off to Scotland with Foxy, an old school friend. Life on a remote croft is hard and the two boys must still face up to the future. What will it hold for them?

David J. Fleming

Now Then, Al

COLLINS

LIONS · TRACKS

First published in Great Britain 1989 by
Lions Tracks

Lions Tracks is an imprint of
the Children's Division, part of
the Collins Publishing Group
8 Grafton Street, London W1X 3LA

Printed in Great Britain by
William Collins Sons & Co. Ltd, Glasgow

For Andrew Skinner and the Skinner clan,
past and present.

1

Alan idly flicked the buttons on the remote control as the channels on the television flickered in front of him.

The pale green floral curtains were half closed to block out the little sunlight that came into the living room of the small terraced house, and the faded pattern of the wallpaper gave the room an even greater atmosphere of gloom than he had already created for himself.

He slowly unwrapped the half bar of chocolate he was holding and ignored the specks that fell to his pullover. The one o'clock news blared into the room. Alan flipped the last piece of chocolate into his mouth and rubbed the silver paper into a ball before flicking it into the fire place. It bounced off the hard brown tiles and gave a "ting" as it hit the gas fire.

The mid-day paper was still spread out on the floor where Alan had left it. The pages were open at "Vacancies" and the pen for circling the adverts was lying next to it, unused.

He heard the back door open and footsteps across the tiled floor of the kitchen as his mother came through, clutching a shopping bag. Her mousey weather blown hair framed her red face as she puffed loudly and glanced disapprovingly at Alan.

"Are you still lounging around here?"

Alan shrugged without looking at her.

His mother continued talking as she let the door close slightly and took her coat off. She put the coat on the hooks at the bottom of the stairs and poked her head back into the living room.

"You should be out looking up college courses or trying to find a job instead of sitting around here hogging the television all day."

"I've just been out for a paper and there's nothing in it," Alan said indignantly.

His mother gave an impatient frown and went through to the kitchen. She raised her voice to be heard as she began emptying the shopping bag.

"If I can get a part time job I'm sure there must be something you can do." She came back to the living room and stood against the doorway with her arms folded. She was still wearing the green overall from the supermarket. "You know what your Dad thinks about you sitting around all day."

Alan sighed heavily as he flipped off the television and turned in the chair so that he could see her better. His broad shoulders were pressed tightly against the back of the chair as he looked at her.

"Look. I keep telling you. I don't know what I want to do."

"You've finished school Alan. You're in the outside world now so you'd better buck your ideas up."

Alan stood up and followed her as she went back into the kitchen and began taking pans from the cupboard.

"Yeah. You keep saying that, don't you," Alan said, "but you don't come up with any better ideas than I've got already. You think it's easy or something? I've just left school with qualifications you can't even count on one hand and you think it's a boom town out there or something."

"Now don't you talk to me like that Alan," his mother said sharply. "You know we're only trying to help. We got Kevin and our Elaine off to a good start and that's all we want for you."

Alan leaned back on the door frame in exasperation.

"Oh for heaven's sakes Mum. You keep saying that. Our Kevin's eight years older than me and Elaine's five years older. Don't you think things have changed a bit since they were looking for jobs?"

His mother heaped some potatoes into the sink from the shopping bag and began peeling them as she talked.

"There's jobs to be had for those that look for them Alan. Things are picking up. You read about it in the papers all the time. There must be something you can do."

"Not round here there isn't."

"What about college then?"

"What about college?"

"You'd better apply if you're going to have any chance of getting in."

"I told you. I haven't got the results I need to do anything decent."

"Well whose fault is that, but your own?"

"Don't start that again."

Alan stepped back as his mother moved him out of the way to get to the chip pan in the cupboard.

"Our Elaine did well at school because she worked hard. Now look where she is. She's got a good job earning good money. You've got no-one to blame but yourself."

Alan groaned loudly. He'd heard the same conversation over and over. Our Elaine this. Our Kevin that.

"Things are diferent now Mum. I'm not sitting around for the fun of it. Just because you've gone back to work after God knows how long, you're flushed with success."

His mother looked up sharply.

"I put a lot of effort into getting that job. There was fourteen other people after that job." She put the chip pan on the cooker and went back to the sink. "And besides, I think I deserve it after bringing you lot up. I've been fastened to this house with no money for long enough."

Alan tried to control his temper.

9

'Yes. But just because our Kevin and Elaine are doing great, and you've just started working again, it doesn't mean everyone's struck gold."

"I never said that Alan."

"There's thousands of people like me. How am I supposed to compete for a job with the results I got?"

"Well, anyway," his mother continued. "Maybe you could get an apprenticeship or something."

"A what!"

"Well our Kevin did."

Alan stared in astonishment.

"Good God Mum. What planet have you been on?"

Mum waved the wet potato knife in the air as she glared at him.

"Don't you let your father hear you talking to me like that my lad or you'll be out on your ear."

Alan shook his head and went through to the hall. He took his black canvas jacket from the hooks at the bottom of the stairs and went back into the kitchen.

"I'm going for a walk."

"Don't you want anything to eat? I was just doing some chips."

"I had a sandwich when I went for the paper."

"Suit yourself."

He wound round his mother in the small kitchen and went out the back door into the yard. His footsteps changed pitch and echoed slightly as he turned up the alley between the red brick terraced houses and came out on to the street at the front.

He put his hands in the pockets of the canvas jacket and walked along the wet pavement with his head down, kicking at bits of stone and empty cigarette packets as he went. He wanted to escape. There was a feeling inside him of dread and uncertainty, as though the city itself were beginning to tighten slowly around his neck. What about a

10

job? What about college? What about money? What about . . . everything.

He took a short cut across a derelict council estate, standing empty and disused, then across the back of another line of terraced houses until he came out on to the main road into town.

He passed the huge Comprehensive school, sitting empty in its tarmac landscape with its gates firmly locked for the Summer. As he passed it a sense of loathing overcame him and relief that he wouldn't have to go back next term.

The rush of air from the traffic pulled at his fair hair as he reached the centre of the town.

He walked to the pedestrian precinct near the High Street. It was full of housewives and kids and office workers rushing for a sandwich and groups of unemployed men standing around. He found a bench seat and sat with his hands in his pockets, watching the people passing to and fro.

The bench was in the centre of the pedestrian area. It had been hacked at with penknives and had graffiti across the back. Alan noted without interest that "Brownloaf is a puff" as he sat down at one end of the bench and stretched his legs out. He scratched at the seam of his jeans where it was rubbing his leg as he watched the mass of people pass in front of him.

He pressed his chin down on to his chest and chewed thoughtfully at his bottom lip. He felt angry, frustrated and confused. It must be someone's fault. The government's fault. His parents' fault. Why didn't anyone seem to know what was going on? Didn't anyone give a damn, or what?

The precinct was paved with different coloured paving stones that had once looked very attractive. Now they appeared faded and drab. On either side of him, surrounding the precinct, were the high buildings of the department stores, with their brash window displays and their endless sales. Chairs, videos, coats, three piece suites. Prices slashed. 10% off all goods. Summer Sale. Only £499.99.

There were strategically placed young trees, inset into the coloured pavement at intervals of five metres. They must have looked wonderful on the architect's plans, but in reality they looked frail and dwarfed by the surrounding buildings.

Little gusts of wind rushed from the doorways of the department stores every now and then and blew a discarded crisp packet around in a scittering spiral, like some sort of twentieth century tumble weed.

Alan hunched his shoulders and bounced the heels of his training shoes against the pavement in a bored rhythm, then he looked up and stopped the movement as he saw a face coming towards him through the crowd.

The young man had his hands in the pockets of his brown leather bomber jacket and walked with his head lowered even though there was a slight bouncing rhythm to his step. His brown eyes were wide and suspicious, peering through the fine strands of long greasy hair that framed his face, as if he expected to be attacked at any minute. His eyes seemed to be too close together and his skin was dirty pale, like someone who'd been in hospital for too long.

Alan smiled wryly. Foxy. Everyone called him Foxy. As he came nearer to the bench the nickname seemed even more appropriate. His eyes flickered nervously around the open square and his head bobbed almost imperceptibly, like a boxer's instinctive ducking. It wasn't hard to imagine him hiding wide eyed behind a hedge watching the hounds approaching across an open field.

"Now then Al. You working?"

"Now then Foxy."

Foxy always said, "You working?" It was a habit he'd picked up from his older brother whose friends were generally unemployed, redundant, or sacked. He now used the expression in the same way someone would say "All right then?"

Foxy sat next to Alan on the bench but barely gave him a glance as he talked. His eyes constantly flickered and focused towards some unknown danger in the crowds of passing shoppers as he dipped his head and peered through his lashes.

"How's it going Al?"

"Rubbish."

Foxy looked at Alan and then laughed as he turned away and began scanning the precinct again.

"Yeah. Me too. I got my results. Know what I got? Zilch. Nothing worth having anyway."

Alan nodded. "I know the feeling."

Foxy pulled the tab end of a cigarette from his breast pocket and cupped his hands to light it with a match. The smoke plumed up off his fist and evaporated in the wind. He breathed it in and looked at the cigarette as if he'd never seen one before, then he resumed his nervous scanning of the horizon. His head moved towards Alan as he spoke but his eyes were elsewhere, never meeting Alan's.

"Billy got done," Foxy said quietly.

"Yeah?"

"Six months community service."

"He had it coming," Alan said without malice. "He's been doing daft things for ages. He's a bit of a nutter. You're better off steering clear of him Foxy. No kidding. He's just trouble."

Foxy nodded as he looked at the fading ember of his cigarette and took a long draw on the filter. He pulled a face and licked the acid taste from his lip then flicked the tab end at a nearby tree. It bounced off the bark and blew with the breeze into a shop doorway.

"Don't know what I'm going to do now man. Not now we've finished the exams and everything." Foxy breathed out heavily. "Suppose I'll end up on one of those government slave gangs or something, making tea for some bloke who just wants cheap labour."

"Me too," Alan said. "And I've got my parents on my back."

"Dave Weston got a job with a building firm."

"Yeah?"

"Yeah. Beats me how it all fits together man. He's more thick than me and he gets a job. And there's what's his name? Glasses."

"Brinkley?"

"Yeah. He got something cleaning offices or something."

"How'd he get that then?"

Foxy shrugged and kicked at a piece of chewing gum stuck to the pavement.

"Don't know. Must know someone."

They were silent for a moment as they watched an old lady with bow legs shuffle across the pavement in front of them.

"Must have been dead easy when my Dad was a kid," Alan said. "They used to just leave school and go straight into a job. No problem. Money and everything. It never even occurred to them that they wouldn't get one. Just a case of which one. Must have been dead easy that."

"Yeah," Foxy said without looking at Alan. His eyes were still on patrol, looking at the people passing by. Had Alan not been at school with Foxy he'd have presumed he was on the look out for someone particular, someone who was after him. But it was just the way Foxy always moved, bobbing, weaving, eyes flitting here and there as if someone was about to leap out and attack him.

14

They'd not really been friends at school. Just the same groups for lessons a lot of the time. But actually leaving school had broken down barriers between people. As if everyone had suddenly grown up. As soon as the exams finished and people realized they wouldn't ever have to go back again, they all started talking to each other. Even people who'd been at each other's throats started an unwritten truce on the final count down to leaving.

"You've not got anything lined up then?" Foxy asked.

"Nah. Not a thing."

Foxy took some chewing gum from his pocket and put a stick in his mouth without offering any to Alan.

"Want to buy some cigs?"

"Oh yeah? How many?"

"Four hundred."

Alan raised his eyes to the sky.

"You been out nicking again?"

"Not so loud man."

"No I don't want your cigs. You know I don't smoke anyway."

"Just thought I'd ask." Foxy stood up and lowered his head as if he was about to say something important. He spread his fingers through his hair to move it out of the way. "Well. I'll see you then. I've got to see a bloke down the market."

"Yeah. See you Foxy. Don't get nicked."

Foxy nodded and walked away up the pedestrian precinct, dipping his head at imaginary threats, his eyes flitting nervously across the faces of people walking towards him. His step had a bounce to it as he thrust his hands deep into the pockets of the leather jacket and hunched his shoulders.

Alan watched him disappear, then left the bench to stroll through the shopping area. He stopped outside a record shop and stared at the new records splashed across the window in an inviting display of colour. He dabbed an index finger on the clean glass and left a smudge as he nodded to himself. That one. That would be the one he'd buy. If he had any money.

He walked past the shops and pubs, past the department stores and public buildings until he reached one of the main roads that spread from the centre of the city, like bicycle spokes, to the outer edges of the suburbs. He knew nearly every step of the road with its small shops and factories. All of them were subtly changing each day, with each walk into town, like the imperceptible drifting of sand on a shore line. A different poster here, a new sign there. Small changes that grew and subsided so slowly that only those who'd been away a long time would detect the difference.

He passed the old Grinding Works. Painted on the brickwork high above the door it said simply, "Grinding Works". The "Grinding" was so dull and flaking that it was hard to tell what it said, and "Works" was covered with a grey mould that camouflaged it against the grubby brickwork.

The red brick building no longer had the side doors open, showing the intense heat and work taking place inside. No more screeching sprays of sparks to watch, or the back and forth movement of the massive machines. No more flasks and sandwiches and blue grease-stained overalls, or finger-marked pin-ups above the machines or the smell of hot metal being cooled with oil.

Next door, a bicycle shop that had only opened six months before was boarded up as if in sympathy with the surroundings. Its sign, still new, looked over dressed and conspicuous against the drab exterior of the other buildings. And next to that was a small newsagent's, with a metal grille across its dirty window, hanging on for dear life.

Alan walked slowly, barely noticing the passing traffic

or other people going about their daily business. He passed the school again and noted with satisfaction that someone had scrawled in felt tip pen across the school sign, "Mr Hucklow is a prat".

He eventually came to his own road and walked down the dim alley between the two houses. At the front door he put a fingernail under a flaked bubble of green gloss paint and flicked it off, revealing the pale yellow underneath. Then he pushed the door open and walked into the kitchen. It still smelled of chips. His mother was back at the supermarket and his father not home yet, so he went up the narrow stairs to his bedroom. He sat on the bed for a moment with his hands in the pockets of his jacket and then flipped over to lie down. He lay there, silent, his ankles crossed. His eyes staring unfocused at the ceiling.

It was all to do with money. Or was it jobs. Money. If you had money you didn't need a job. If you had a job you had money. If you had qualifications you could get a job. If there were jobs. There weren't any jobs. There wasn't any money.

He felt a pain in his jaw and realized he was grinding his teeth. He held out a hand and looked at the outstretched fingers. They were shaking. Only slightly. But they were shaking.

It had started before the exams. Hardly noticeable at first. Just a feeling of tension and irritation. A feeling of vague dread. A dread of the future and what he was going to do. A dread of working or not working or signing on or not signing on. Of passing his exams. Or not.

Just a constant unexplainable dread.

2

Foxy and Tony passed the Grinding Works, peered carefully around the deserted street and looked at each other nervously in the orange glow of the street lights. Behind them a high wall surrounded the back yard of the Newsagent's and half way along that, was an equally high wooden gate.

Across the top of the wall and gate was a tangled spiral of corroded barbed wire, which had collapsed under the weight of its own rust, leaving a clear access across the middle of the wooden gate.

They looked round one more time and scrambled silently up on to the top of the gate. They vaulted over into the dark shadows on the other side and crouched down, waiting expectantly as the gate swung back on its hinges and creaked.

Tony was older than Foxy and had an angular face. His nose was pointed and had a slight bump on the bridge. The street light caught his nose and sharp cheek bones, causing shadows across his eyes and giving him a ghoulish appearance. His eyes stared intently into the gloom of the back yard as he silently pointed to a small window, half a metre square, at the back of the building. Then he made his way stealthily through the crates of empty pop bottles towards it and signalled that Foxy should follow.

Foxy followed him and crouched below the window feeling his heart beating inside his leather jacket. He parted his lank hair with both hands as it fell over his eyes and watched with interest as Tony produced electrical tape from a plastic carrier bag.

Tony stuck long strips of tape from the top of the window frame down across the window. Strip after strip, just a few centimetres apart. When the window was striped with the sticky tape he lifted his arm and back elbowed the glass. There was a sharp crack but no sound of shattered glass.

The two of them froze in the darkness and waited without daring to breathe, but no other sound came. Tony began peeling the tape off the top of the frame pulling with it the pieces of glass as they dangled free. He urged Foxy to move out of the way and lowered the pieces noiselessly to the ground.

Foxy silently pulled an empty plastic crate over to the window and stood on it so that he could get his arm round the jagged remnants of glass and unfasten the window catch. Tony held the window open as Foxy heaved himself head first through the small opening. He balanced for a moment, his legs sticking straight out behind him as his eyes adjusted to the darkness, then holding on to the window sill he slithered in a twisted somersault so that his legs followed through the window on to the floor of the shop. When he had righted himself he took the torch offered by Tony. It had a sock pulled over the end of it to dim the light.

Foxy peered into the gloom of the stock room as he made his way between the boxes of sweets and cards and bundles of magazines. He found the cigarettes in the corner of the room and began bundling the packets into a plastic carrier bag. When the bag was full he handed it through the window to Tony.

"Hurry up!" Tony whispered at him through the opening.

Foxy glared at him in the glow of the torch.

"What do you think I'm doing!"

He went back into the room and filled another carrier

19

bag and after handing it to Tony he pulled himself back on to the sill and out into the back yard.

"Come on. Let's get lost."

They made their way quickly through the crates, holding a carrier bag each and with one movement clambered on to the top of the high wooden gate. In that instant they both saw the same thing and froze in different states of imbalance. The gate clanged noisily on its hinges as it swung under their weight.

The policemen sitting in the parked car on the other side of the road were as surprised to see them as Foxy and Tony were to see the car. They didn't react immediately but stared wide eyed at the two figures as they swayed on the gate, then Foxy recovered and yelled.

"Run!"

He leapt off the gate and ran at full speed away from the police car, not looking back and yet knowing from the screeching of brakes and the shouts that Tony had been caught. Foxy shot up a garden path, down the side of the house, and across two back gardens as the sound of running feet pursued him. He ducked down behind a small bush and waited wide eyed, as the silhouette of the policeman came into view up the side of the house. The policeman paused for a while peering into the darkness of the back gardens, then he suddenly turned and ran back to the police car.

Foxy set off running again, his eyes piercing the darkness as he leaped over another garden fence and shot across the lawn down to the alley between the two houses. He peered cautiously round the corner of the building and seeing that all was clear, raced across the road and down the alley between the houses opposite.

He pressed himself tightly into the darkness of the wall as the police car, with Tony in the back, cruised across the end of the alley. Suddenly the roar of a car being driven at high speed could be heard and another police car screeched down the road and pulled up opposite the first. Windows were wound down and Foxy could hear low voices and the sound of the police radio inside. Both cars set off at high speed in opposite directions leaving Foxy pressed against the wall.

He began running again, through the alley and into the back yard of a terraced house. He came up to a wooden fence at the end of the yard and scrambled up and over as the loud bark of a dog pierced the quiet. More running. Across the road. Out into the derelict housing estate and across broken bricks and a dangerous array of debris until he could duck down into the shadowy safety where two walls met.

He wheezed noisily and spat as he crouched on the ground holding his winded side. He wiped his mouth and breathed deeply trying to get the oxygen back into his body.

All the time his eyes scanned the road, the walls, the houses. His ears were listening for anything, everything, his head ducking instinctively at imaginary danger. Then his breathing began to slow and steady and very cautiously he raised his head and peeked round the side of the wall. The street lights cast deep shadows over the derelict houses as they stared back with black eyes for windows. The bricks lay in the street like an aftermath of a riot, but all was quiet.

Foxy peered round the wall, up towards the main road and then half crouching, half running, made his way across the housing estate to the bright lights of the main road. He tucked the plastic carrier bag under his jacket as best he could and walked briskly towards the centre of town, heading for a pub he knew.

The pub had long since shut its doors and all the customers had drifted away to their various homes. The bar was in darkness but there was a single light on in the upstairs bedroom. Foxy looked up and down the street and knocked loudly on the heavy wooden door. He waited for a moment and knocked again.

A thin beam of light showed through the etched glass window of the door as the landlord came down from the flat upstairs. The figure came near to the door and called through to the shadow on the other side.

"What do you want?"

"It's me!"

There was a slight pause.

"I don't care who it is. We're shut."

"It's me! Foxy!"

"Foxy?"

"Let me in Jack. Quick."

The locks on the door grated loudly and then it opened a fraction. When the landlord saw who it was he opened the door wider and let Foxy slip inside.

"What the hell are you playing at coming here at this time of night?"

"I had to Jack."

Jack narrowed his eyes and bolted the door shut. He was a big man with a massive pot belly. He moved his hand over his balding head to sweep the long strands of hair back into place.

"What you playing at Foxy?"

"I got some stuff for you." Foxy held out the carrier bag to Jack. He took it silently and peered inside.

"Are you stupid or what? What the hell're you getting me out of bed for? You'd think it were the crown jewels or something." His eyes widened fractionally. "You just nicked these?"

"Yeah. Right, but look, see . . ."

Jack ducked and looked through the clear part of the etched window.

22

"What if someone saw you eh? What're you playing at?"

Foxy held up his hands to calm Jack.

"It's all right. It's all right. Nobody saw me."

"They'd better not have or I'll kill you myself."

"Nobody saw me Jack. Nobody. Don't worry."

The big man breathed out noisily through his nose and stared at Foxy.

"You do this again and you're in bother."

Foxy ducked nervously like a boxer and kept glancing through the window.

"Yeah. Right. O.K. So what will you give me?"

Jack opened the bag wider and held it to the glow of the street lights coming through the window.

"Thirty quid."

"What!"

"Do you want it or not?"

"There's got to be a hundred quids' worth there at least! Come on Jack. Please."

"Thirty. Take it or leave it."

"Bloody hell Jack."

"Thirty."

Foxy sighed heavily and bobbed from one foot to the other.

"All right. All right."

Jack turned to hide a grin and thrust his hand into the deep pockets of his trousers. He produced a fistful of crumpled ten pound notes, peeled out three, and gave them to Foxy.

"Ta."

"Now bugger off and don't come back with stuff in the middle of the night unless you want us both nicked."

"Yeah. Right. Ta."

The locks on the door were opened and Foxy slipped out into the night and disappeared into the shadows. He kept near to the wall as he smiled to himself and walked towards the centre of town.

3

Alan's father rested the small tobacco tin on his knee as he took a pinch of tobacco from the tight brown wad. He put it on the cigarette paper and teased it out with his fingers as Alan's mother waited for him to continue.

The television was actually off, indicating that what he had to say was serious. Once he'd got the tobacco in position he rested his elbow on the thin covering of the arm chair and began to roll the cigarette. His face was strained.

The gas fire hissed loudly in the silence as he stretched out his legs on the mottled green carpet and bent forward to pick up the lighter from the coffee table.

The small ligaments beneath the skin of his thick wrists flicked a few times as he struck the lighter, then he breathed in the smoke and blew it out in a sigh. The picture of the "Crying Boy" above the fire place stared down at him as he glanced across to Alan's mother.

"I don't know love. All I know is that they're laying off six."

Alan's mother looked across at him.

"There's been rumours like that for months love."

"I know, but this is different."

"Has someone actually said something this time then?"

Alan's father nodded as he sat up in the chair so that he could lean forward and rest his elbows on his knees.

"Carter came down from the office and gathered us round. All he knows for certain is that there's going to be six fitters and four turners laid off in the next month. After that they don't know."

"And they haven't said who?"

"No."

"So you might be all right?"

Alan's father blew out a thin stream of smoke and retrieved a strand of tobacco from the end of his tongue.

"It's usually last in first out. Unless it's management, then they make up their own rules."

Alan's mother ran her fingers through her hair and went across to sit on the arm of the chair. She put her arm round her husband's shoulders and rubbed them as if he were a child that was cold.

"You were there before John and Andy and Pete. There must be more. You've been there six years now. They can't just get rid of you like that."

"They can love," Alan's father said. "That's the trouble." He leaned back in the chair. "Anyway, at least we've got your money from the supermarket. And if Alan gets off his backside we might be all right."

Alan sat down on the end of the bench in the bus shelter and picked at the lukewarm chips cupped in the paper. He ducked as a chip flew in his direction from one of the other boys in the group.

"Now then Riggy!"

Riggins and Pete laughed and sat down on the bench.

"It were bad that."

"Well chuck it somewhere else then."

"Now then Al," Riggy said as he began poking around in the chip packet. "You seen that Sharon since we left?"

Riggins was only slightly older than Alan, but already a dark line shadowed the top of his lip where the fluff of a moustache was beginning to show. He'd also become muscular over the last year and he showed off his new

25

found manliness by wearing a T-shirt with the sleeves cut off.

"Well?" Riggy repeated. "Are you still knocking her off or what?"

Alan glowered at him.

"Mind your own business Riggy."

"She were with that whatisname from Highgate," Pete said as he delved into his chips. "I saw her yesterday."

Pete was tall but ungainly, as if his legs had decided that he should be a basket ball player but the rest of him hadn't agreed yet. Alan looked at him and back to the greasy paper.

"So what if she was with someone?" Alan said. "What's that got to do with me then?"

"I thought you were knocking her off," Pete said. "That's all."

"Well I'm not."

"You're not now anyhow," Riggy said and choked on his chips with the amusement. He got up and spat a huge gob of chips into the road, then came back and sat down. "She's off out with that bloke from Highgate."

"Anyway," Alan said as he screwed his chip paper up and tossed it under the bench, "you've got room to talk."

"How do you mean?"

"What happened with you and Julie Wilson at that party."

"That were nowt."

"Like hell," Alan laughed.

"What?" Pete said as he looked from one to the other. "What happened then?"

"She poured a drink over his head."

"Did she hell!"

"She did then!"

"Did she?" Pete said as his eyes lit up. "When?"

"At that party."

26

"You shut up Al. You don't know what you're talking about," growled Riggy.

They went suddenly quiet as two girls came round the corner and into the bus shelter.

Alan grinned when he recognized them.

"All right Julie?"

Julie was the taller of the two. She wore a black leather jacket, short black flared skirt and black tights. Her normally mouse brown hair was jet black and her lips a despairing dark purple.

Her friend, Carol, trailed behind her, dressed in a similar fashion but her timid slouch and pale face only made the outfit look ridiculous.

"All right Alan?" Julie said. "Has Sharon been out?"

Alan shrugged. "Why ask me?"

"Beg my pardon," Julie said sarcastically. "I thought you were supposed to be going out with her."

"No."

"Just thought," Julie looked at Riggy and pulled a face. "I see you crawled out of the gutter then?"

Alan and Pete suppressed a laugh as Riggy scowled.

"Oh shut up you tart!"

"Don't you talk to me like that you fat slob or I'll pour another drink over your head!"

Riggy stood up.

"Come on Pete. I'm off. I'm not hanging around here."

Pete began stuffing chips into his mouth.

"Hang about!"

"Are you coming or what?"

"All right. All right."

Alan smirked as the two girls moved out of the way to let Riggy and Pete pass.

"See you Riggy."

Riggy didn't reply. He just glanced over his shoulder

with what he hoped was a withering look and disappeared round the side of the bus shelter, followed closely by Pete.

"He's a fat slob," Julie said loud enough for them to hear, then she sat down on the bench followed by her silent shadow, Carol. "What have you been doing then?"

Alan shrugged. "Just hanging about here."

"There's nothing to do round here. It's a hole this place," Julie said as she kicked the rolled up chip packet further under the bench with her heel. "We went to the Barleyman but they wouldn't serve us."

"Yeah. I tried that one," Alan said. "It's no good."

"You got anything sorted out then?"

"How do you mean?"

"Jobs and that. I've got on a hairdressing course."

"Yeah?"

"Yeah. And Carol's signed on for a cookery thing. You know, chefs and that."

Alan looked at his training shoes and tapped them on the floor a few times.

"No. I haven't got anything sorted out yet."

"You'll have to hurry up or you'll have to do a YOPS. Right waste of time that is."

"Not if you get a job after."

"Some chance. Anyway, I'm doing a hairdressing course. There's always jobs for hairdressers."

"You think so?"

"Yeah. My Dad says there's always jobs for hairdressers. You've only got to look in magazines. Everyone has to have their hair done."

"Yeah," Alan said quietly. "Maybe." He stood up and put his hands in his pockets. "Anyway, I'm off. I'll see you around."

Julie looked up at him. "Shall I tell Sharon I've seen you?"

"What for?"

"I just thought . . ."

"Give over. I'm not going out with her."

Alan turned his back and left the bus shelter. He spent the next few hours wandering the streets near his house. He knew it would depress him but he didn't care. Inside him there was a strangled sensation as if something were trying to break free. But nothing happened. Nothing changed to relieve the sense of hopelessness he felt.

When he got back to the house the sound of the television greeted his arrival. There was a smell of fried food and wool too close to the fire. His parents were still up, watching the television with the lights off and not a word between them as his father's nicotined fingers rolled another cigarette and his mother ate biscuits from the tin by the fire. Alan flicked the light on as he entered the room.

"Turn the light off Alan!" his father said without even turning from the screen.

"How can you see? It'll do your eyes in."

"Do what your Dad says."

The light snapped off again and Alan pushed his way round the settee and sat on the end, feeling like a late arrival at the pictures.

"Can you lend me five quid Dad?"

His father looked over.

"No I can't. I gave you some money only yesterday."

"I put it towards some trainers."

"Tell us after this," his mother said irritably. "It'll be finished soon."

Alan stood up suddenly from the settee and clenched his fists with anger.

"Why don't you ever listen to me!"

"Sit down Alan and act your age."

"You don't give a damn about me do you! You don't know what's happening do you? I haven't got a job and to

29

you it's as if nothing's happening! I'm sick of it. You never listen to me! You still think I'm a kid."

Alan flicked on the light switch at the door.

His father turned in the seat and glared at him.

"Well you're acting like one. Turn the light off for heaven's sakes."

"Turn it off yourself!"

Alan slammed the door and strode noisily upstairs.

"Alan!" his father's voice shouted up the stairs. "Come down here!"

Alan slumped down on the bed and put his head in his hands.

"Come down here!" the voice shouted again.

Footsteps thudded up the stairs and ended with the bedroom door being flung open.

"What the hell are you playing at eh? Just what the hell are you playing at coming back here and dictating to us?"

Alan's voice was quiet and strained.

"I wasn't dictating to you."

Alan's father took a step forward.

"You don't tell me what to do in my own house lad or you're out! Our Elaine and Kevin didn't cause this big fuss and disrupt the whole house so I don't see why we should put up with it from you."

"I've tried to explain but . . ."

"You're too old to be acting like a child so don't come clever in our house." His father moved into the centre of the room, his anger distorting his face. "And it's about time you started looking for a job or a college course or something. Our Elaine didn't spend weeks moping about the house. She got out there and got things done."

Alan could feel the anger tightening in his chest. Always the same argument.

"I don't know what I want to do!"

"Don't you shout at me lad!"

30

"I wasn't shouting. I was just telling you. But you never listen."

"Well I'm not having it in my house."

Alan thumped the dressing table to redirect his anger.

"You don't listen to me! You just don't care."

His mother's voice could be heard at the bottom of the stairs.

"For God's sake you two keep your voices down. You'll have next door complaining again."

Alan's father turned on him.

"You get yourself sorted out or you're out. Don't think you can sponge off us forever. We're not made of money you know."

Alan stared at his father. At that moment he hated him. But the hatred melted into a loathing and he turned away.

"Do you hear me?"

Alan didn't answer. Frustration and anger were too near the surface for him to dare to speak. His father waited a moment and then nodded as if to a puppy that had been slapped and finally got the message. Then he walked out and slammed the door.

Alan sat on the bed. Why couldn't they understand? He'd tried to explain but there were no words to describe his feelings. Every day it was the same. The same frustrations and lack of communication. As if his parents had used up their allotted amount of tolerant understanding on Elaine and Kevin and now just wanted to be left alone.

He stood up and looked in the dressing table mirror. It showed his own stern face looking back. He was sick of it all. Sick of the town. Sick of the lack of hope. Sick of being useless and misunderstood. Sick of the likes of Riggy and the grime and the smell of living in a dead city.

Dust drifted from the top of the wardrobe as he pulled his haversack from under the junk piled across it. He could hear the bass of the booming television drifting from below

31

as he took some clothes from the chest of drawers. He found the bundled sleeping bag in the bottom of the wardrobe and crushed it down into the haversack.

There was no anger now. Just a cold blooded realization that he needed to get away. He had to get away from the house and his parents so that he could think.

He could feel the tension round his neck and chest. He watched his fingers and saw them shaking. He felt like crying and the tightness across his chest and throat made him feel sick.

Alan found the small amount of money that he'd saved at the back of his chest of drawers and put it in his pocket. Thirty four pounds. That was the lot. He'd need to work out how he was going to manage with such a small amount, but right now all he wanted was to be away.

He went down the stairs quietly and opened the door to the darkened living room. The lights were off and the television over loud. His father and mother were still watching the flickering screen as if it were the only thing that gave them life.

"I'm going."

His father looked up.

"Eh?"

Alan took a deep breath and looked from his father to his mother.

"I'm going."

His father watched him for a moment and made to stand.

"Look, I'm sorry Alan . . . I've got problems at work and . . ."

"I'm going."

"And where are you going at this time of night?"

Alan walked to the door and turned.

"I just thought I'd tell you."

"Well? Where are you going?"

"I'm going job hunting."

And then he was gone. Out into the street.

He walked quickly. Away from it all. His parents. The lack of jobs. The lack of money. The hopeless future. All of it. He just wanted out. He walked methodically. He knew where the motorway was.

The deserted streets and the litter in the gutters confirmed his loathing. The whole city was dead. Like the Grinding Works and the bicycle shop. He could breathe at last in the knowledge that he was getting out, even for a short while, away from all this hopelessness.

Alan reached the centre of the city as the nightclubs were spewing out drunken revellers. He walked past the crowded taxi rank and out through the main streets until he came to the road leading to the motorway. Then from behind him came a familiar shout.

"Now then Al!"

Alan looked behind him and saw Foxy bounding along the pavement with his hands still deep in the pockets of his leather jacket. He looked even more pale than usual in the glow of the orange street lights. When he caught up with Alan he grinned broadly.

"Now then Al. You working?"

Alan gave a weak smile and continued walking up the road as Foxy bobbed along beside him.

"All right Foxy."

"Where you off at this time of night?"

"Just getting away."

Foxy faltered in his stride and then caught up with him.

"You what?"

"I've had enough. I'm just getting out for a bit."

As Alan and Foxy walked, they began to pass the empty buildings of the closed down steel works. A huge avenue of red brick. Gate six. No Unauthorized entry.

"Where're you going then?"

Alan thought for a moment. Then he had it. He knew.

33

"Scotland."

Foxy's eyes widened and he laughed.

"At this time of night man? There must be better places to be than Scotland?"

Alan shrugged. "Seems like a good idea."

"What's in Scotland then?"

"My Great Uncle."

"Oh yeah?"

"He's got a croft. He's my Grandad's brother. He's got a croft in the North of Scotland."

"Seems a long way to go man."

"I told you. I've had enough. I just want to get away."

Foxy went quiet for a moment as they continued walking then he pulled at the sleeve of Alan's jacket as he stopped in front of the next gate. Gate eight. No Unauthorized entry.

"Now then Al. How about me coming?"

Alan looked at Foxy. He didn't want company. He just wanted to get away from everything. He didn't even really know Foxy. Why should he want his company?

"You?"

"Yeah. Go on man. It'll be a good laugh. I haven't done anything daft for ages. Going to Scotland sounds a laugh. We can stay at my place tonight and then take off tomorrow. You aren't going to get a lift at this time of night are you?"

The two of them stopped and Foxy waited as Alan thought about it.

"Are you sure you want to come?"

"Yeah man. 'Course! I've never been to a croft thing and I could do with getting away from this dump for a bit. It'll be a good holiday."

"What about your parents? Won't they mind me staying the night."

"Don't be daft," Foxy grinned. "I live with my brother

34

in his flat. My parents gave me the push ages ago when I had trouble about that car."

Alan lowered his eyes and tapped his foot thoughtfully.

"I've not told anyone I'm coming. I don't know if it'll be all right for both of us to go. I haven't been there for years. Are you sure you want to come?"

"Yeah. Go on. It'll be a laugh. I'll come with you to Scotland anyhow. I might go off on my own after that but it'll be good to get away."

Alan smiled. To hell with it.

"Well . . . Yeah. I suppose so. Where do you live?"

"I'll show you."

Alan followed Foxy as they wove their way up through the back streets and eventually came upon a high rise block of council flats. They entered the building.

"Lift's knackered," Foxy explained as they began the long climb up the stairs.

The walls were covered in graffiti and spray paint and a strong smell of urine filled the darker corners of the stairs where the light bulbs had been smashed or stolen.

They reached a dark blue door at the fifth landing and Foxy fumbled in his pockets to produce a bundle of keys.

When they entered the flat there was a smell of damp air and sweaty bodies. Then Foxy found the light and they entered the small living room.

"My brother's gone off somewhere. Don't know where he is but he won't mind anyway. Make yourself comfortable."

Alan looked round the living room. It was strewn with clothes and records out of their sleeves. He moved to the settee and politely moved a pile of jumbled clothes further up the cushion.

"Here I'll shift that," Foxy said as he bundled the pile of jeans and socks into his arms and threw them to the other side of the room with another pile of linen.

"Do you want a coffee Al?"

"Yeah. Ta."

Alan felt suddenly sad as he looked round the grim flat. The atmosphere was cold and damp as if no-one really lived there. He glanced up as Foxy called to him from the small kitchen.

"Do you want sugar?"

"Yes. Just one thanks."

As Alan looked at the room, he felt Foxy's whole life was there for him to see. The dirty clothes. The dinner plate in the fire place with brown sauce smudges round its outer edge where it had been wiped with a piece of bread. The ash trays full with tab ends and the records strewn against the wall and record player.

A coffee cup sat in the fire place surrounded by sticky rings, forming the shape of a distorted Olympic symbol.

"How long you been living here then?"

"Eh?" Foxy stuck his head round the door as the sound of the electric kettle began to rumble in the kitchen.

"How long have you lived here?"

"About a month. Our Terry's O.K. He isn't here most of the time so there's no bother. Just as well really. I've got nowhere else to stay since my Dad threw me out."

Alan began to feel sorry for Foxy. They'd never really been close friends, but now he felt for him, on his own in a damp flat.

The sitting room curtains were still open and as Alan stood up he could see the whole city spread out in front of him with its orange lights blazing in the distance, threading strands of light across the ground like a cobweb covered in dew.

"You can doss on the settee Al," Foxy said as he came back into the room carrying two cups of coffee.

"Ta."

Foxy gave Alan a cup and put his own down in the fire

place. He sat on the crumb strewn floor and lit the gas fire with a box of matches as he talked.

"So where's this croft thing then?"

"It's in the North of Scotland."

"How long will it take then? To get there?"

Alan shrugged. "I don't know. It's a long way. Two days maybe."

"What about sleeping?"

"I hadn't thought really."

Foxy took a stub of a cigarette out of the full ashtray and lit it.

"That's no worry anyway," Foxy said as he studied the end of the cigarette. "I've got a sleeping bag. Best take a couple of bin liners in case we have to sleep out somewhere. Have you got a map?"

"No."

"Best take Terry's AA map then. I'm looking forward to this. I've never been to Scotland."

"You been hitching before?"

"Yeah. Loads of times. Not been that far though. Not all the way up there, but I've dossed about a bit sometimes. Last summer I went to Cornwall and slept on the beach."

"Yeah?"

"Yeah. It was freezing. And the police at Newquay moved me on in the middle of the night. I ended up in a shop doorway huddled against some hot air grille thing. Actually it wasn't bad that. Once I got comfortable. Should be a laugh this. I'm looking forward to it."

4

In the morning the two of them made their way from the flat to the motorway feed road on the outskirts of the city. Foxy still wore his thin leather jacket but he had bundled a pullover and some spare clothes into the white sports bag he'd used at school. They'd started early and it was only eight o'clock when they reached the huge roundabout leading on to the motorway.

Cars passed occasionally but without a hint of stopping as Alan held out his thumb. A few lorries slowed as they passed, but it was an illusion. They were simply changing gear to prepare for the long upward haul on to the motorway itself. Then a long continental truck humped through its gears and growled to a noisy stand still just a few metres up from them. Foxy shouted "Yeah!" and ran towards it. Its indicator blinked rhythmically as Alan and Foxy ran along the hard shoulder and finally came level with the huge cab, vibrating noisily with the engine.

Alan put a foot on the wheel hub and pulled at the door, then climbed in with Foxy close behind. The driver shouted over the noise of the engine as they both shuffled on the long seat with their bags between their knees.

"Where are you going lads?" he asked as he fought the lorry into gear.

"Scotland."

The driver raised his eyebrows slightly and laughed. "I can't do you that much, but I'm going to Newcastle if that's any good."

"Yeah, great."

The driver pointed to the door with his thumb.

38

"Pull it again. I don't want you falling out."

Foxy pulled hard on the door and it clicked as it shut properly. Alan put a thumb up to Foxy as the driver looked in the side mirror and pulled the huge lorry on to the slip road. The low growl of the engine changed in pitch and then they were on to the motorway, gliding down the inside lane, high above the ground with the white lines streaking below them.

They moved further from the city, passing the outlying industrial areas and the railway goods yard with its long snakes of coal trucks. The dark sandstone buildings gave way to red brick houses and modern housing estates and then they were in open country, passing rugged dark green fields.

The huge cab breathed power and was warm in the early morning sun. Foxy twisted himself to look in the side mirror.

"What are you carrying?"

The driver looked across as the gears changed and the cab found its resonant frequency. It hummed loudly and died away as the revs increased.

"What?"

"What are you carrying?"

The driver smiled. "Toys."

Foxy laughed. "Yeah?"

"Dolls. Thousands of them."

"Doesn't fit the Yorkie bar image somehow."

The driver shrugged. "One load's the same as the next. I've just got to deliver them that's all."

"You done this long then?" Alan asked.

The driver looked in the side mirror and pulled out past a slow moving lorry.

"About five years."

"Do you like it then?"

The driver looked across to the side mirror on Foxy's

side of the cab and waited for the lorry behind to flash its lights, then he flicked his own lights in a thank you and pulled back into the inside lane.

"Yeah. It's a good job. Nobody getting on your nerves telling you what to do every five minutes. I like it. I've done all sorts of jobs before this. Buses, taxis, the lot . . . What do you two do then? Are you students?"

Foxy laughed loudly so Alan gave him a sideways look and turned to the driver.

"No. We just left school."

"Yeah? You look older. What are you going to do then? College?"

Alan shrugged. "I don't know yet."

The driver dipped his head slightly as he looked in the mirror again and overtook another slow vehicle.

"Mind, it's a bit bad up here for jobs I suppose."

Foxy nodded. "You can say that again. Especially when you haven't passed your exams."

The driver smiled.

"You didn't do so well then?"

"I got nothing worth shouting about that's for sure man."

"You could take them again at college."

"Yeah," Foxy said. "I could if I wanted. But all I want to do is earn a bit of money. I don't want all that college stuff. All I want to do is do some work and get proper money for it. You wouldn't think it'd be that hard to do, but it's nearly impossible up our way."

The driver nodded but he gave the impression that he was lost for words. He concentrated on the road until Alan spoke.

"You don't know of any do you?"

"What's that?"

"Jobs. Do you need anyone for unloading? That sort of stuff?"

40

The driver shook his head.

"Can't help you there. We do all our own unloading. Or the people at the other end organize it for us."

Alan shrugged and leaned back in the seat. The driver noted his depressed expression.

"Is that why you're off to Scotland then? Job hunting?"

"No, not really," Alan said quietly. "It's just a sort of holiday. Anyway it's probably just as bad up there for people our age."

They went quiet then, all lost in their own thoughts. A couple of hours later they came to the outskirts of Newcastle and the lorry pulled over to the side of a roundabout in a hiss of air brakes and flying grit.

"I'll drop you here lads. You'll get a better lift from here than if I take you into Newcastle. If I drop you in the town you'll have to walk all the way out again."

They thanked the driver and climbed down from the cab, dragging their bags with them. The lorry engine roared and ground the gears as it moved off back on to the roundabout.

"That wasn't bad eh Al?" Foxy said as he looked at his watch. "Took us three hours. We could be in Scotland this afternoon if this keeps up."

They walked further across the roundabout and stood next to the sign which said "North". It was covered in graffiti and scratched with names from the many hitch-hikers who'd also stood next to it trying to get lifts. Littered around the base were empty coke cans and discarded crisp packets.

An hour later Foxy was swearing and sticking two fingers up at the cars who wouldn't stop.

"Give over Foxy!" Alan shouted at him. "Someone might stop and come back to belt you one."

"They're just selfish!" Foxy cursed as another half empty

41

car glided past them and down on to the motorway. "You'd think I were the Boston Strangler or something."

"Lay off, would you!"

"Well, make one of them stop then."

"They might do if you stop mucking about."

Alan could feel his anger rising. He was stuck with Foxy whether he liked it or not, but he was beginning to wish that he hadn't let him come along.

"Stop it now Foxy!"

Foxy's outstretched hand dropped to his side. He glared at Alan and stepped back from the edge of the road.

"All right. All right man. Keep your hair on."

"I'm just saying, that's all."

"I heard you."

Foxy moved away from the hard shoulder and unzipped the sports bag. He took out a Mars bar and had just taken a huge mouthful when a rusty Cortina pulled up next to Alan.

A thin man with black glasses and a dark suit leaned across and wound down the window.

"Where are you going boys?"

Alan opened the door and put his head inside.

"Are you going North? We're off to Scotland."

The driver nodded and leaned over the back seat to move various pamphlets and advertising leaflets out of the way.

"I'm going into Edinburgh. Is that far enough?"

Alan looked behind him to where Foxy was zipping up the sports bag.

"Come on Foxy."

"Mmmm Hmmmm," Foxy said as he nodded and clambered into the back of the car, chewing away to clear his mouth.

Foxy settled in the back of the car and Alan in the front, then they set off down the feed road to the motorway and picked up speed.

"On holiday are you?"

"Yeah," Alan said, "just going to visit a few relatives."

The man looked at the sky thoughtfully.

"You've been lucky with the weather. It's pretty unpredictable the further North you go. Still it's been nice all this week."

Foxy took a brief look at the advertising leaflets and moved them further up the seat. There was nothing worth stealing. He stretched out and closed his eyes as they coasted along the motorway. In the front, Alan and the driver talked politely.

After an hour they were all silent. Foxy was deeply asleep in the back of the car, hunched up on the seat. Then as they approached Jedburgh the driver looked across at Alan.

"So are you friends then?" the man asked as he looked in the rear view mirror to see Foxy slumping against the door frame.

"Yeah, sort of. We used to be at school together."

The man nodded to himself and checked the mirror again. His forehead was perspiring slightly.

"Your relatives expecting you are they?"

Alan looked across. He suddenly felt a rush of blood to his face as his heart beat faster. There was an unnerving feeling of danger. The man seemed to be nervous and kept sitting high in the seat so that he could look at Foxy in the rear view mirror.

"Er . . . yeah," Alan quickly lied. "Well . . . yeah. They are, yeah."

The man nodded and remained silent for a moment. He swallowed and flicked his eyes in the mirror again.

"Have you got anywhere to stay tonight? Are you staying in a hotel or bed and breakfast?"

"Well er . . ." Alan said uncertainly. He felt threatened

but wasn't sure why. They were perfectly innocent questions but there was something about the man's tone of voice that made him feel wary.

"We've not decided yet," Alan said and had a quick look over his shoulder to see if Foxy was awake. He was still fast asleep in the back of the car with his head resting in his hand as it vibrated against the window.

"You're welcome to stay at my place if you like. I often have people to stay. It'd be no bother."

Alan swallowed.

"No. No thanks. Thanks but . . . we're expected somewhere."

The man looked across and smiled lamely.

"I see."

They were just moving on the ring road around Jedburgh when Alan took the opportunity to escape. Something felt sinister and he wanted out.

" In fact you can drop us here."

"What?"

"Can you drop us here?"

The man frowned. "I thought you were going to Edinburgh?"

"Well, yeah . . . but Foxy wanted to see Jedburgh. He likes to look around these places. Never been this far North see."

The man shrugged.

"Are you sure?"

"Yes," Alan said as he swallowed nervously. "Yeah. Just here's fine . . . No, just here. That's great."

The car pulled up at the verge just outside Jedburgh and Foxy woke up because of the sudden quiet.

"Eh? You what?" Foxy said as he opened his eyes sleepily and looked around.

"We're getting off here Foxy."

"Eh?"

"Come on."

"Where are we?"

"We're getting off here."

"Oh yeah. Right."

The two of them got out of the car and then Alan thanked the man and began walking quickly away. The driver looked at them in the mirror. He put the car sharply into gear and sped off down the road.

Foxy rubbed his eyes and looked around him.

"Where's this then Al? I thought we were off to Edinburgh."

"That bloke was a bit funny."

"Eh?"

Alan cast a finger in the vague direction of the car.

"That bloke."

"What bloke. Where are we?"

"We're just outside Jedburgh."

"That in Scotland then?"

"I don't know. Listen," Alan said as he dumped his haversack on the verge. "While you were asleep he started asking things."

"Eh?"

"He asked if my relatives were expecting us. Then he said we could stay the night at his place."

Foxy stared at Alan and then creased his eyebrows.

"So?"

"Don't be so naïve man. He was weird."

Foxy looked up the road in the direction the car had just gone then looked back at Alan.

Foxy stared at Alan and then creased his eyebrows.

"So?"

"He was after us . . . You know."

Foxy looked up the road in the direction the car had just gone then looked back at Alan.

"No kidding?"

45

"Yeah."

Foxy watched Alan's face to see if he was joking and then burst out laughing.

"And I missed it. I wished I'd seen that. I bet your face was amazing man."

"It isn't funny!"

"He wouldn't have done you any harm man. There were two of us."

"Shut up Foxy. It was scarey. He was looking really weird and he was sweating like he was nervous. He might have had a knife or something."

Foxy laughed louder. "Give over man. He was only a weedy little bloke."

"It wasn't funny. Anything could have happened."

"Like what?"

Alan sighed and turned away.

"Oh shut up and stick your thumb out."

Foxy looked at Alan's stern expression and turned to face the oncoming traffic.

"Come on Al. Loosen up man. We're on holiday."

They waited another twenty minutes and then a car pulled up next to them. The young couple in the car were driving to Pitlochry in Scotland and were quite happy to give Foxy and Alan a lift.

They eventually stopped for a meal at a service station on the other side of Edinburgh, just before the Forth Road Bridge, and watched the traffic moving like ants across the bridge as it spanned the Forth estuary. Next to the road bridge was the Forth Rail bridge, crossing the deep water with its spectacular dark red girders.

Alan pointed to the rail bridge as he sipped his coffee in the shelter of the service cafe.

"It takes fifteen men three years to paint from one end to the other of that bridge. And then they start all over again."

Foxy stared at the bridge.

"No kidding?"

"Not really," Alan said and took another sip of his coffee, "I just made it up."

"Do you reckon they might be looking for painters?"

"Don't be daft."

"Anyway," said Foxy, "I don't like heights."

By late afternoon they were winding their way slowly towards the Grampian mountains. The huge hills rose high above the road on either side, showing off their deep greens and browns as the low evening sun highlighted them.

Foxy and Alan sat quietly in the back of the car, numb with travelling and stiff from sitting so long, until the two of them were nodding in a semi-sleep and longing for the end of the journey. Even the beauty of the surrounding countryside couldn't cheer them as they shuffled their legs and tried to ease the ache in their cramped knees.

Late at night they eventually entered Pitlochry. The young couple let them out, wished them luck, then drove away as they wandered, dazed and tired, on the outskirts of the town. The town was quite small and very quiet. There was no sign of life other than the occasional glimpse of light coming through the curtains of the road side houses.

"I'm freezing man," Foxy said as he hugged the leather jacket to himself and stood by Alan on the main road.

"We'd better find somewhere to doss Foxy. I'm knackered."

The two of them looked up and down the road and then Foxy pointed to a hill rising in the distance away from the built up area of the town. It was a forest area high on a hill.

"I think we'd better head up that way. We can sleep in the woods no bother."

Alan grimaced. "That's miles and it'll be wet."

"No. We've got bin liners and stuff. Let's set off in that direction anyway," Foxy said and began walking away.

They both pulled their jackets tighter round them and set off at an angle from the main road, down a smaller road that led into a valley. They passed under a railway bridge and left the houses behind them as they came out in what appeared to be a large car park surrounded by trees.

Alan peered into the darkness as they made their way into the thickest part of the trees.

"What's this place then? It's like a water works place or something."

Foxy shrugged and continued winding his way deeper into the trees.

"Beats me man. But this'll do. We're out of the way here."

When they were in the darkest part of the small wood they pulled their sleeping bags from their haversacks and clambered into them. On top of that they pulled the black plastic bags. The blanket of leaves and moss on the floor cushioned them from the hard ground and soon they had settled down and were quiet from exhaustion.

Foxy lit the stub of a cigarette and could be seen dimly by Alan as the red glow illuminated his face in the darkness.

"Don't set us on fire Foxy."

"It'll be all right man. Everything's damp."

"You said it'd be dry."

"Yeah, well."

They were silent for a moment, then Alan broke the silence.

"Can you hear water?"

Foxy listened. "Sounds like a river or something. Must be in the valley."

Foxy pointed up between the dark outlines of the trees at the sky. The clouds drifted in clumps of black and every now and then a cluster of stars would show through. "Look at that man. Brilliant."

Alan looked up at the stars and pulled the sleeping bag tighter around himself in the darkness. He was tired and cold.

"Yeah. Brilliant."

Foxy's plastic bag rustled as he turned to see Alan better.

"You know something Al?"

"What?"

Foxy stubbed the cigarette out.

"You aren't half a moody git."

"Cheers."

"Well you are."

Alan turned to see Foxy.

"I just need a holiday."

"Well that's what we're here for man."

"Yeah."

"You still going out with that Sharon?"

"No."

Foxy went quiet for a moment and turned over to try and get comfortable.

"Did she give you the push then?"

"No."

"She did."

"How do you know?"

"Riggy told me."

Alan sat up. "It's none of his business!"

Foxy laughed. "Aha! A weak spot me thinks."

"Leave off Foxy."

"All right man. I was only joking. No skin off my nose . . . men never understand women. Not worth trying."

"The great philosopher speaks."

"It's right man. I reckon they come from a different planet."

"Maybe they think the same about you."

49

Foxy went quiet for a long time, then turned over and looked at Alan.

"I never thought of that."

"What?"

"Do you reckon we're as weird to women as they are to us?"

"Maybe."

"I never thought of that."

"Go to sleep."

There was a long silence, then Foxy's mumbled voice drifted from the depths of his sleeping bag.

"No man . . . We can't be *that* weird."

5

Alan rubbed his face as he slowly came to his senses. His left leg was numb with the cold and his hair was plastered to one side of his head where the wet grass had pressed it flat. He slithered out of the damp sleeping bag and wiped his hands in the dew, then rubbed them over his face as he groaned.

He looked across and saw that Foxy had gone. A flattened area of grass showed where he'd been and on top of it was the white sports bag. Alan looked around and saw the darkened area of grass where Foxy's foot prints lead to the car park, then he bent and straightened out his sleeping bag. The plastic bin liner was full of condensation. It crackled noisily as he pulled the two apart and rolled them up, then he crouched for a moment, with his arms crossed in front of him trying to rub life into his cold limbs.

The sound of footsteps crackling on the twigs nearby made him look up. As he did so, the footsteps stopped. A few more steps were taken and the silence was broken by a worried voice.

"Al?"

Alan breathed a sigh of relief and shouted back in the direction the voice had come from.

"Foxy?"

The footsteps started again.

"Where are you Al?"

"I'm here."

Foxy's face appeared through the cluster of trees. He

grinned when he saw Alan huddled on the ground rubbing his arms and legs.

"It was a bit cold man. I couldn't sleep."

"Where've you been?"

Foxy grinned and winked as he held up the bottle of milk that he'd had behind his back.

"Breakfast."

He proudly pulled from his pockets four Mars bars and a packet of biscuits, and piled them on to the sports bag. Alan looked at the food and then frowned at Foxy.

"I'll bet you didn't buy any of that."

Foxy shrugged. "Who cares?"

"I do."

Foxy looked at him. "Do you want anything from this lot or not?"

"Yes."

"Well shut up moaning then."

Alan frowned and opened the packet of biscuits as Foxy took a huge gulp of milk.

"Where did the milk come from?" Alan asked as he prised the biscuits from the packet.

"I nicked it from a cow," Foxy said happily. "This cow were just standing there. So I nipped up behind it and swiped a bottle."

"Oh yeah?"

"Well . . . Someone had left it on a doorstep so I thought I'd better take it in case someone stole it."

"Terrific," Alan said sarcastically.

"I've just had a look round," Foxy said. "We're right in the middle of some public park thing. There's a river down at the bottom over there and this huge dam thing. It goes right across the river in the bottom."

'See," Alan said. "I said we were in a Water Works place."

"No," Foxy shook his head. "It's a park or something."

The two of them ate their Mars bars and biscuits and then packed the sleeping bags and made their way back through the car park.

"See what I mean?" Foxy said as he pointed to a pay kiosk. "We're in a public park or something."

They walked through the car park and up the hill back to the main road through Pitlochry. After looking up and down the road a few times they set off in the direction they believed to be North. The town's main street was straight and very picturesque and although it was still early in the morning there were already a few locals and tourists wandering around, looking in the shops.

The shops and buildings were clean and made from a yellow sandstone which looked even more yellow as the sun shone up the street. They passed the open door of a small baker's shop which let the smell of freshly baked bread drift out on to the street. Near that was a wool shop with patterns of Arran pullovers in the window.

Foxy stopped at a shop displaying guns and tweed hunting clothes. He looked briefly at the window display, at the tweeds and tartans. Alan was striding off ahead of him so he jogged until he caught up and walked alongside with his sports bag banging rhythmically against his legs.

"Just how far is this croft place man? If we go any further North we're going to end up in Iceland."

Alan scratched his head. "We should be there by . . . well this afternoon sometime. If we get good lifts."

"I hope it's worth it."

"It'll be O.K. You'll see."

They trudged quietly along the pavement and then Foxy frowned and pulled the map from his sports bag. He was studying it when Alan came back to see what he was doing.

"I thought something were funny," Foxy said irritably. "We're going the wrong way."

Alan looked closely at the map.

"Are you sure?"

"Yeah," Foxy said and pointed to a metal sign fastened to a lamp post. "Look at that sign there. 'Salmon Ladder'. That's not on the map. We want to be going to Inverness."

Alan laughed. "A Salmon Ladder's not a place you berk."

Foxy stared at Alan and then at the sign.

"Well what is it then?"

"Well it's like . . . so that . . . well it's not a ladder as such. It's a sort of . . . a jump thing. So that salmon can get from one place to another when they go up stream to lay eggs and stuff. You know, when they go up stream to mate."

"I see," Foxy said, "so this salmon hangs about at the bottom of the river and then he sees a female salmon and says, 'Hold on a minute love, I'll just get me ladder'."

Alan shrugged. "We want to be going that way anyway."

"I know where we want to be going."

"Well that's the wrong way."

"Are you sure?"

"'Course I'm sure."

They kept walking until they came to the outskirts of Pitlochry, then they took it in turns to stand with their thumbs out. Eventually a van pulled over and bumped on to the side of the curb as they grabbed their bags and ran after it.

It was only a small transit van so they both had to squeeze together on the front seat. Alan told the driver where they were heading and within seconds they were travelling again.

The driver was a young man wearing a white T-shirt and jeans and he had a cigarette burning unnoticed in his left hand as it held the wheel. His other arm was resting casually on the edge of the rolled down window as the breeze ruffled his hair.

"You on holiday?" the driver asked.

Alan nodded. "Yeah. More or less."

"You camping are you?"

"No not really," Alan said as he tried to get comfortable on the seat. "I'm going to see some relatives on the East coast."

"Aye," the driver nodded. "There's some nice places round there when you go further North. What's the place called?"

"Tiener."

"Tiener?"

"Yeah."

"I've not heard of that."

"It's just outside Dalstrath."

"Oh yes. I know that. Very nice little town. I can't take you that far though. I'm only going as far as Inverness but it'll give you a good start to your journey."

They fell silent as they travelled further North and eventually came to the magnificent Grampian mountains. The road wound its way through the valleys, climbing higher and higher towards Aviemore. On either side of the road the huge mountains stretched into the distance. On the tops of some of them were small patches of snow showing bright against the dark shale and heather. In the distance on the hill sides, dark green and purple with heather, sheep grazed on the rugged slopes.

Small rivers ran by the side of the road, meandering through the valleys, some brown with peat and some clear and bright, twinkling in the sun as the water slewed between the boulders.

At one point the road ran parallel to the main railway line. They watched as a train slowly glided through the valley and caught up with them. As it passed, Foxy waved at the train like a member of the Royal Family and laughed out loud when a small child waved back.

"Wonder where they're all going?" said Foxy.

"On holiday," Alan said.

"Yeah?"

"Well I suppose so."

"Wow," Foxy said as he stared after the train, "it's going to be bloody crowded on this croft thing."

6

"This is Dalstrath," Alan said as he and Foxy walked through the small town, on their way towards the top road to Tiener. "We're only about five miles away now."

Foxy nodded without looking at Alan. Alan noticed that Foxy had gone very quiet over the last part of the journey and wondered what was wrong.

"You O.K., Foxy?"

"Yeah," Foxy smiled. "Just wondering what your Uncle's going to say that's all."

"It'll be all right."

Foxy didn't look like he agreed but he kept quiet as they continued walking through Dalstrath.

The town was a typical small Scottish town, with sandstone buildings and small neat streets that wound in between the shops. In the windows of the shops were post cards of Dalstrath, tartan shortbread tins and occasionally a small doll in full Highland dress. A single High Street cut directly through the centre of the town and on the land behind the shops was the small community of houses. Very little traffic came through this area because of the modern ring road so the quiet town was now left to itself and the few tourists who ventured off the main road.

The sea breeze was blowing small tufts of cloud across the sky as it swept up behind the town and across the land. As they walked further on to the top road and away from the buildings, huge dark patches of shadow could be seen careering across the fields before them.

"I haven't seen a kilt yet," Foxy said.

Alan looked at him.

"Don't tell me that's why you're fed up."

"Don't be daft man. I'm just saying that's all. It's like going to Russia and not finding vodka. I haven't seen one kilt since we've been in Scotland."

Alan smiled and continued walking as Foxy followed behind. They carried on in near silence for the five miles to Tiener. The road was known as the top road because it followed the ridge of land which skirted the sea. It was narrow and virtually deserted with fields running on either side of it. The edges of the road were lined with thick spiky gorse bushes, covered with bright yellow flowers and on the long stretches they could see mirage puddles caused by the warm air drifting up off the tarmac.

The sea could be clearly seen to their left where the land gently rolled down to the shore a quarter of a mile away. Dotted sparsely throughout the fields between the road and the shore was a handful of stone farm houses.

As they began to climb a small rise in the land, the village of Tiener came into view. They carried on a little further until they met a junction cutting at right angles to the top road.

"There." Alan pointed to the white signpost at the top of the village road. Its white paint was peeling but it said clearly in black letters Tiener ½. "This is it."

Foxy looked at the signpost and then down at the village. His head bobbed nervously and then he stopped as Alan continued forward.

Alan looked back and saw Foxy clutching his sports bag and looking anxiously into the distance.

"What's up?"

"I don't want to go man."

"What?"

Foxy shuffled uncomfortably and his eyes blinked rapidly as he dipped his head with his usual nervous movements.

58

"They're your relatives Al. I don't know them and they don't even know you're coming."

"Don't be daft Foxy. It'll be all right."

Foxy shook his head.

"I don't feel right Al."

Alan waited a moment and then walked back to Foxy.

"What's up? You're with me. It'll be all right."

"I just don't want to, man. That's all. I wouldn't feel right staying in someone else's house. It's all right sleeping out and getting lifts and that. But . . ." Foxy paused as if stumbling to find the right words. ". . .I just wouldn't feel right in someone's house man. I'm going back to Dalstrath."

Alan grabbed his sleeve as he turned.

"Come on Foxy! I can't leave you in the middle of Scotland on your own. We're on holiday. What would you do? Where are you going to go?"

Foxy shook his sleeve.

"Leave off Al. I'm just telling you that's all. I just wouldn't feel right that's all."

"But why?"

"I just don't want to. All right?"

Alan looked at Foxy and realized he meant it. He looked at the village and then back again, feeling torn between the two of them.

"So what are you going to do?"

Foxy shrugged. "I'll just have a look around. See where I can doss for a bit and then go back home."

"What about me? We're supposed to be on holiday."

"You'll be all right. You've got all those relatives you keep going on about."

Alan breathed out heavily and scratched his head.

"Come on Foxy. No-one'll do you any harm."

Foxy ignored him and began walking away.

" I told you man. I'm off back to Dalstrath."

Alan threw his bag to the ground and shouted at Foxy's back.

"Oh come on Foxy!"

"No. I mean it."

Alan waited for a moment and then called after him. He picked up the bag and kicked a pebble irritably.

"Well it's up to you . . . But look, if you change your mind just come down into the village and ask for me. All right? It's only a small place so you'll find me O.K. Everyone knows Alistair."

"Yeah, right."

"All right? If you get fed up you'll come looking for me?"

Foxy nodded. "Yeah, right. See you anyway. I'm off."

Foxy turned and began walking along the top road back to Dalstrath as Alan watched him go. He felt sad watching him walking away on his own but knew that he couldn't change Foxy's mind.

As Foxy's head disappeared from view over the rise of the hill, Alan turned back and headed down the road towards the village. As he approached, the light colour of the house roofs showed brightly against the grey blue of the sea behind them.

The small village of Tiener on the East coast of Scotland, sat next to the shore in the ever changing weather blowing off the North sea. The majority of the houses were small cottages, built from the local sandstone and white washed in the traditional manner. But on the outskirts of the original village were signs of new developments. More modern houses had sprung up with pebble-dashed walls and angular shapes.

The whole character and history of the village had been built from farming the surrounding land. Even so, the crofts were now not big enough to support the inhabitants and the younger people were constantly moving out to get work further afield. Only a small handful of crofters still worked the land around the village.

A road wound round the end houses of the village, following the line of the shore and then cutting at right angles to the sea. It meandered slightly as it moved up the small incline of the land and stopped at the top road to Dalstrath.

Half way between the top road and the village was a small cluster of sheds and shearing pens. These, and the surrounding fields, were Alistair's croft.

Alan looked back at the distant shape of Foxy as he disappeared from view, then walked down the road towards the village. He saw the small sheds on the croft and an estate car parked by the gate. The air smelled fresh, of flowers and grass and the sea. As he walked he breathed deeply through his nose like someone who'd just come out of a smoky room into the cool air. The clouds were drifting across the sky in huge balls of white, casting dark and light patches across the fields as the sun shone through the gaps between them.

A man was attending to sheep in a far field. Alan narrowed his eyes slightly to focus on the distant figure and smiled. Alistair was easily recognizable, even though Alan had only been a small boy when he was last in Tiener. He remembered how Alistair used to let him sit on the tractor, while he ploughed a field or turned the hay. And he remembered Alistair giving him an old flat cap to wear. It was far too big, but he'd worn it anyway, proud that he looked like his Uncle, a "real" farmer.

As Alan went through the five bar gate next to the road and walked up past the shearing pens he could feel excitement building up inside him. The familiar smell of the fields and the sight of the croft helped him recall the feelings of his childhood, when he was free from worries about jobs or exams.

He walked through the yard and past the barn, before climbing through the wires of the fencing into the field with the sheep. Alistair was walking with two sheep dogs by his side and he turned when the smaller of the two dogs barked at the approaching stranger. The dog bounded towards Alan at such an alarming speed that he thought he was going to be attacked. He backed off a step but she just ran round him in excited circles and occasionally made an attempt to leap up on him.

"Rona!" Alistair shouted after her, "Rona! Come here! Leave the man alone now!"

Rona ran back towards Alistair as the two men walked towards each other. Alan smiled, seeing the familiar shepherd's crook and the friendly craggy face of his Great Uncle, with the flat cap perched on his head just as it always had been. The other sheep dog followed in Alistair's footsteps weaving back and forth as they crossed the field.

"Hello Uncle Alistair."

Alistair frowned slightly, trying to place the young man's face. He smiled back but began to apologize.

"I'm sorry son . . ."

Alan laughed and interrupted him.

"It's me. Alan. You're my Great Uncle."

Alistair's face broke into a wide smile.

"It's Alan! Well I'll be . . . I didn't recognize you. What on earth are you doing here? I didn't recognize you. The last time I saw you, you were just a wee boy." His voice was loud and friendly as they walked towards the yard with the two dogs circling around them. "It's good to see you boy. What brings you to Tiener after all this time?"

Alan shrugged. "I just needed a holiday, so I thought I'd come up here."

"Well it's certainly a surprise. And how's your father and mother? Are they with you?"

"No, no. They haven't come up. They're O.K. though."

"Och well, they'll be busy no doubt. It's good to see you though. Where are you staying?"

Alan swallowed, embarrassed by the predicament.

"Well, actually, I haven't really sort of worked it out. I just thought I'd come up and see everybody."

Alistair looked puzzled but he said nothing. He was pleased to see his Great Nephew. He could still remember tiny Alan following him around the croft in his new red wellingtons.

"Well you're welcome Alan. You can stay with me for a day or two if you like. It won't be luxury mind and you'll have to sleep on the settee I'm afraid."

Alan nodded enthusiastically. "That's great! I won't be any bother."

"Aye well. Come on now. We'll call in on Maggie, that's Stewart's mother, and have a wee cup of tea. You'll not remember Stewart but he gives me a hand now and then."

The two of them strolled through the yard and down to the estate car, with Rona and Tam chasing each other round their legs as they walked. Alistair herded the two dogs into their compartment at the back of the car as Alan opened the side door and climbed in. The car smelled of seaweed and sheep dogs and there was a fine layer of sand on each seat.

"Did you come up by train?" Alistair asked as he took his place in the driving seat.

"I thumbed a few lifts. Only took two days."

When Alistair started the car the two dogs in the back jolted and then stood up again as they tried to poke their noses through the bars, excited by the presence of a stranger.

Alistair looked in the mirror.

"Sit down will you!"

The two dogs shuffled as the car changed gear and eventually contented themselves with looking out of the back window as the car moved down the narrow road into the village. It was exactly as Alan remembered it. Just a small collection of single storey bungalows clustered next to the sea and raised from the beach by only a few feet. The smell of fire wood and salty air brought childhood memories flooding back.

The tide was out leaving a wide expanse of wet sand, mottled with seaweed and mussel beds.

As they drove up to the house the two dogs began shuffling excitedly and then Alistair led the way from the car with Alan following behind. He stamped his boots hard outside the house and removed his cap as he ducked through the low door.

"Maggie. I've got a surprise for you."

"I'll be with you in a minute," Stewart's mother called back from the kitchen.

Alan waited for Alistair to remove his boots in the hall and then followed him through to the living room. He looked round briefly and sat nervously on the end of the settee.

"Is Stewart no' here Maggie?" Alistair called through.

"No. He's away to Dalstrath but he'll not be long."

Stewart's mother finally came through from the kitchen and noticed the stranger. She paused for a moment in the low doorway. She was a big woman with huge arms that were folded over her flowered blouse.

"And who's this you've brought with you Alistair?" She looked closely at Alan for a moment and raised her eyebrows in surprise. "It's not wee Alan surely?"

Alan grinned, pleased by the recognition. He nodded.

"Well goodness me. You've grown." She looked at Alistair as he made himself comfortable in the armchair. "You should have told me there was someone coming Alistair." Then she turned to Alan. "And how's your Mam and Dad? Are they up with you?"

"Er, no . . . I came up on my own."

"You'll have to tell them to come up and see us. It's so long since they were here. Is this a flying visit then?"

Alan shuffled uncomfortably. "Well I'm not sure really. Just a few days."

Alistair's strong voice easily filled the small room.

"Aye. He's staying with me for a wee while. I've told him it's not the Ritz but he's quite welcome to stay."

Maggie suddenly held her hands in the air.

"Listening to me blethering. I haven't even asked you if you want a cup of tea."

"Aye that'll be fine," said Alistair.

"I might've known *you'd* be wanting one."

Alistair and Alan were plied with tea and various scones, biscuits and cakes. When they had chatted and Alistair had smoked a pipe the two of them took their leave.

Alistair's house was at the end of the main street of low cottages. It was white washed like the others and had a slightly overgrown front garden with a shed at the end of it.

At the front door was a heavy two pronged sea anchor that had been painted black and placed next to the porch for decoration. Alan smiled when he remembered that he'd been smaller than the anchor the last time he'd seen it. Now it only came up to his waist.

Alistair let the two dogs out of the car and hustled them into the small wooden shed at the bottom of the garden. As Alan passed it, he lowered his head to look through the small door and noticed how dark it was.

"Do they stay there all the time?"

"Aye. You can't have working dogs as pets Alan. They don't work properly. They get lazy."

Alistair bolted the shed and walked up the path with Alan. When they reached the front door Alistair simply pushed it open and walked in. No-one locked their door in Tiener.

Alistair placed his cap and working jacket on the hooks in the hallway and then went through into the living room.

"I'm sorry I can't offer you a bed, but I got rid of the other one after Rosy died. You can sleep on the settee if you don't mind. Or you could maybe stay at Stewart's if I asked."

"No I'm fine," Alan said quickly. "Honestly. The settee's O.K."

He followed Alistair into the dim living room. It was cold compared to the warmth of Stewart's house where the fire had been attended all day. The remnants of last night's fire lay grey and uninviting in the cold grate.

"Bit chilly at the moment but I'll soon get a fire going. Sit down son and make yourself at home. You can watch TV if you want to."

Alan placed his bag behind the settee and sat for a moment studying the room as Alistair went off into the kitchen. It was quite obvious that Alistair had lived alone for some years. A pair of slippers lay at angles in the middle of the floor. The morning paper was open on the dusty dining table with a half empty tea cup glued by a sticky ring to its pages. Next to it was a pair of reading glasses, sitting where they had been left that morning.

The ceiling was low as in most cottages, but it made the room feel cosy and safe. The settee and arm chairs were solid square shapes with floral patterns. The pale brown curtains were sun faded, giving a feeling of permanence in spite of their drabness.

Alan stood up and went to the fire place. Hanging on the chimney breast were two leather harnesses displaying a collection of original horse brasses. He remembered that they'd belonged to the horses used by Alistair's father.

A photo of Alistair's children and late wife stood in a

silver frame on top of the television. Great Aunt Rosy had died more then ten years ago. Alan never knew what it was she'd died from, but he remembered his parents' hushed conversations after a late night phone call, and the way the conversations always ended as soon as he came into the room.

"Can you make the fire up Alan?" Alistair called through over the sound of water filling the kettle.

Alan looked towards the kitchen.

"Er . . . yeah."

He hadn't made a fire since he was about eleven years old. He'd made fires among the derelict houses that had finally been demolished to make way for a supermarket. He and his best friend used to steal potatoes and roast them in the ashes, then go home and wonder at their parents' uncanny ability to know they'd been playing with fires. The fact that their faces and hands were black and their clothes stank of wood smoke hadn't occurred to either of them.

Alan knelt in front of the brown tiled fire place and reached over to some old newspapers stacked by the fire. To one side of them was a copper bin filled with kindling sticks and coal. He screwed the paper into loose balls and laid them in the fire place, then he placed the kindling wood on top like a boy scout's fire.

As he worked a sense of peace came to him. A sense of coming home.

7

Stewart walked out from the village and set off up the road to the croft. He'd just finished his "A"levels and was spending the Summer in Tiener before going to University. He'd always helped Alistair whenever he could. He'd earned pocket money occasionally, but he did it more for the pleasure of working on the land and doing something useful with his time.

Stewart was tall and well built, with dark red hair. He looked tough, like the land around him.

Half way up the road he came to the five bar gate that led into the croft. As he climbed the fence and began walking past the shearing pens, a ginger farm cat followed him. It padded along the tractor tyre ruts in the mud and then veered off to rub itself sensually against a fence post. The wooden shearing pens were green from the lichen and moss that had grown on them in the damp air. Beyond them were the open yard and farm sheds.

Various pieces of machinery, among them a harrow, a seeder and a baler, were lined up round the yard like a collection of forgotten military weapons but each one had a purpose and was known by Alistair down to the last nut and bolt. Under the tarpaulin sheets their coatings of chipped paint could be seen marking their years on the croft like the rings on a tree trunk. They looked neglected, but nothing could be further from the truth. Alistair would walk around for weeks with a nut and bolt or specially made bracket in his pocket, knowing exactly what piece of machinery would be needing it.

The sheds were ancient and made of a collection of

planks and corrugated iron. They had been built by Alistair's father and they still stood against the cold sea wind and rain as if they weren't aware of their insubstantial structure. They were weathered and matured and part of the land in the same way that Alistair was.

Beyond the sheds stood the new open barn, looking bare and vulnerable without its bellyful of hay. The tall open-sided structure seemed hollow and strangely neglected, but it would have its purpose when the time of year was right.

As Stewart crossed the yard, Alistair appeared in the doorway of the end shed. His weathered face broke into a smile as he pushed his cap back on his head. He had the complexion of a man who lives by the land and, although his face was reddened by the wind, his eyes shone brightly underneath the greying eyebrows.

"I thought you'd be along Stewart boy. I've got a wee job for you."

Stewart smiled. No matter what Alistair said when he came up to the croft it always included "I've got a wee job for you".

Alistair had a piece of baler twine wrapped round his fingers. It was tough coarse string used for fastening the bales of hay and was nearly as hard and unyielding as the palm that held it. Like all farmers he was forever collecting bits of it or fastening something with it. He unravelled the string and placed it in the pocket of his woollen jacket as he began to walk away.

"What's the job then Alistair?" Stewart asked as he followed.

"Nothing much really," said Alistair, "I'm just going to give one of the ewes some medicine."

Stewart knew that it didn't need two of them to give a ewe medicine but he was also aware that Alistair liked his help.

"O.K. Which one are we going to do?"

"You see the ewe by the fence?" asked Alistair.

Stewart looked and saw several ewes standing by the distant fence. It was always like this, as if Alistair knew each sheep individually and expected everyone else to know them as well.

"Which one?"

Alistair spoke as if only the blind couldn't have seen it.

"That one there. The one with the funny leg." He looked at Stewart to see if there was any recognition, "the one with the two lambs."

Stewart stared hard. There were several sheep with two lambs.

"Och well. You'll see," Alistair said as they walked across the yard to the sheds. As they went in they were met by a musty smell of hay and old sacks. Two old shepherd's crooks hung on a nail on the wall with their curled ends tied to their stems with binder twine so that they wouldn't unfurl in the changing atmosphere of the shed. Various cardboard boxes containing nails and tacks and small screws were stacked on the end of a bench and empty fertilizer bags were piled neatly in the corner next to a pair of hand shears. Above them an old farm jacket hung from a nail, and next to that, on a small shelf, was a brown ale bottle containing the medicine.

"Away for the dogs now," Alistair said cheerfully, hitching up the belt on his trousers as he strode down the side of the shearing pens towards the green estate car parked by the gate. The old horse head brass buckle on the belt eased its way slowly down again, pulling the thick leather with it until the belt lay on his hips exactly where it had started.

At the approach of their master the two sheep dogs in the back of the car went wild. The grille across the back of the car rattled as their tails beat on the roof and the metal work. When the back door swung up the dogs launched themselves at Alistair in a lunatic frenzy of scurrying circles and leaps.

Tam, the older of the two dogs, had a greying muzzle in spite of his vast energy. He was a Collie by pedigree and had sharp features softened by rusty brown fur and the white bib on his chest. Rona, the other dog was a young bitch of dubious background but the sheep dog in her was obvious. She had a black straggly coat and keen brown eyes that shone with enthusiasm.

Without any instruction Rona launched herself through the gap in the wires of the fencing and disappeared as fast as a greyhound towards the sheep.

Alistair watched for a moment, then his eyebrows creased in frustration and he bellowed at the distant dog.

"Come to heel here!"

Stewart wanted to laugh but stopped himself in case Alistair saw him. He had seen this happen so many times. Tam, the older of the two dogs would stay close to Alistair, watching his every move, whilst Rona would leap off and circle the nearest sheep whether she was supposed to or not.

"Rona! Rona! Will you come unto heel!"

Alistair bellowed as he always did. To anyone who had not heard it before the Scottish accent bent the words into "Cammanta heel". It rolled off the tongue and was easier to shout than the conventional "Come to heel".

"Cammantaheel!" Alistair shouted again. "Will you cammanta heel here!"

Rona dipped and stopped and stalked and ran around the confused gathering of sheep. She then hared across the field and zzzinged through the fence at lightning speed towards Alistair's voice as he bent to retrieve his shepherd's crook from the back of the car.

Alistair raised his crook as if to hit her, but in a fraction of a second the dog was well out of reach, looking back with a "What did I do?" expression.

"Now heel will you!" Alistair said sternly.

Rona's big nervous eyes watched him as she skulked close by, dipping her head and lowering her shoulder at his every move. Alistair moved slowly towards her and patted her on the head, then ruffled the front of her chest. He sighed like an exasperated parent as the dog panted loudly and wagged its tail.

"You're a silly thing aren't you? Eh?"

The dog wagged her tail harder and appeared to agree.

As Alistair looked up he saw Alan walking up the village road towards them. He smiled and turned to Stewart.

"Ah, here's the new boy."

Stewart frowned and turned to Alistair.

"Is that Alan? The one my mother was saying about?"

"Aye. He's come up for a bit of a holiday."

Alan smiled as he came up to them. He nodded a hello at Stewart and turned to Alistair.

"You should have woken me up."

"Och no boy. You looked like you were in need of the rest. Did you get some breakfast?"

"Yeah. I found the stuff you'd left out. Thanks."

"We're just going to give a ewe some medicine right now," Alistair said. "If you just follow with Stewart you'll not be in the way."

Alistair and the two dogs walked back up to the yard and out to the far field as Alan and Stewart followed behind.

"Is it a while since you were here then?" Stewart asked.

"Yeah. I used to come up here when I was a kid but I've not been for ages. I was about seven the last time."

"You come by train?"

"No. I thumbed it."

"Good grief!" Stewart exclaimed. "How long did that take?"

"Well. We were . . . I was lucky really. It only took two days."

Once they were in the middle of the field Alistair pointed to Rona.

"Heel now."

Alan watched with interest as Tam, the older dog, readied himself for action. Alistair looked at Tam. The dog looked up. Lean. Ready. Eyes bright. Tongue wet in anticipation. He reminded Alan of a sprinter ready at the starter's block.

"Away Tam."

Tam's powerful shoulders hunched at the neck and sprung back like a catapult as the back bone and hind legs pumped across the field in a smooth rhythmic curve.

Alistair followed in the trail of the dog as it bounded across the springy grass. He held a hand up to his eyes and shouted.

"Go by. Go by now."

Tam veered across the ground with the smooth curve of a jet fighter and instinctively slowed as he approached the left flank of the bunching flock.

"Lie down!"

The dog quickly crouched, like a wolf about to pounce, and trod step by step, belly down, slithering towards the sheep. Ears pricked. Tongue hanging. Never looking away.

"Lie down Tam!"

Down he went, ears up, eyes unblinking, the shoulders hunched. Flat to the ground. Watching. Watching. Listening on the wind for a command. A look back to Alistair. What now? What now? Watching the flock. Ears scanning. Shuffling forward on his belly. Tongue out. Closer.

"Away here!"

Away he went, smoothly to the right across the back of

the sheep as they fumbled in a lost group away from the corner of the field.

"Lie down!"

The sheep settled. Nervous. Watching the dog. Protecting their lambs. Spreading out in a gradually widening line across the front of the dog, as he lay in the grass. Panting. Waiting.

Alan was spellbound. He remembered seeing Alistair and his dogs working together when he was a child and he'd seen sheep dogs on television. But to see it now, right in front of him, held a kind of magic. There was a dream quality to it all, as if Alistair and Tam were reading each other's minds and neither of them could act unless it was in harmony.

Alistair judged the moment when most of the sheep had spread out between him and the dog.

"Come through! Come through!"

Tam fast-walked through the flock, his high shoulder blades mimicking his legs as the lowered body brushed the grass and the fur ruffled across his spine. As he went through the flock the sheep scattered left and right. Tam moved slowly through, tongue hanging, eyes left and right. The flock moved away round either side of him.

"Lie down now! Lie down!"

The two splintered parts of the flock drifted as if by momentum away from the dog as it lay still, between them. Panting. Waiting.

Alistair, in the meantime, had been walking up the field towards the sheep with Stewart and Alan, Rona weaving an energetic trail behind them with her tongue hanging out. Alistair was concentrating on the business at hand, scanning the flock.

"Away here!"

Slowly, Tam moved the eight sheep that had been

74

separated from the flock, down the right side of the field. They began to trot. To panic zig zag. Too close. Too close.

"Lie down man!"

Down went Tam as the sheep continued foward, looking to each other for support and moving into the corner of the field.

The fencing nearby suddenly gave a zzzing and the sheep scattered like marbles as Rona shot between them and began chasing the nearest one. The rest of the sheep panicked and began buffeting the fence trying to get away. Alistair pulled his cap from his head and threw it to the ground.

Alan grinned. The young dog had suddenly reminded him of Foxy. It was exactly the sort of thing Foxy would have done.

"Ya stupid animal! Cammanta heel here!" Alistair bellowed.

Tam looked up, confused.

"Cammantaheel will you!"

Tam started trotting back, bewildered by the change in tactics as Alistair's voice carried across the field.

"Not you! Lie down Tam! Lie down Tam!"

Tam lowered himself on the grass so quickly it looked as if he'd been shot.

"Rona! Come to heel!"

Rona looked reluctantly back at Alistair and then broke off from the chase. She darted like a bullet across the field to her master. Bright eyes. Tail wagging. Tongue hanging out. How did I do?

Alan thought of Foxy again. The dog was acting just like Foxy had when he'd stolen the milk. "How did I do?" Foxy's expression had said when he'd pulled the bottle from behind his back.

"Ya stupid wee scallywag!" Alistair said.

Rona backed off, surprised at the reaction.

"Just what am I going to do with you young lady?"

Rona looked up. Her shoulders dipped low as her eyes widened and her ears pricked.

"Anymore of this young lady and there'll be no more coming up to the croft. Hear me?" Alisair's voice softened as he saw the comic expression on the dog's face. Rona was listening with her head cocked sideways. She watched every expression on his face and wagged her tail now and then to see if that's what she was supposed to do.

Alistair petted the dog as the tail thrashed in the air.

"I don't know," Alistair said to Alan, "maybe she's a bit young yet."

He tied a piece of binder twine to her collar and looked up the field to the still prostrate form of Tam, waiting patiently for the next command. The small group of sheep were still in the corner of the fencing so Alistair instructed Tam to move closer so that they'd stay there. Then he and Stewart and Alan walked up the field towards them.

When they were quite close he fastened Rona to a fence post and he walked towards the sheep in the corner of the field holding out his crook at an angle, with his arms spread wide.

As the sheep bolted along the line of the fence he reached out with the crook and hooked it around the neck of the sheep he wanted. Its front legs lifted off the ground momentarily as it jerked against the pull of the stick, then Alistair quickly moved forward and grabbed it. He let the crook drop to the ground and reached over the top of the sheep to grab its front legs. It stood perfectly still for a second and then struggled to escape, but Alistair had his arm wound firmly round its neck.

He swung the sheep away from the fence and heaved its front legs upwards as he took a step back. The sheep tottered ludicrously for a moment and then its hind legs crumpled and it sat down on its rump with all four legs

76

sticking out horizontally. In that position Alistair could jam the back of the sheep between his knees and hold it steady.

Stewart walked towards Alistair as he placed a thumb and finger at either side of the ewe's mouth, in the middle of the jaw where there was a gap in the teeth. With pressure applied on the fingers the ewe's mouth opened in a grimace and bared its grass stained tongue.

Alistair gave Stewart a nod.

"Off you go now boy."

Alan stayed back out of the way as Stewart gave the bottle a wipe across the top with the cuff of his jacket and placed it carefully between the ewe's teeth. The ewe bucked and gagged but Alistair had its mouth jammed open. It prised its tongue up and down against the roof of its mouth trying to push away the bottle then it gagged and swallowed until all the liquid was gone.

Alistair released the sheep. It shook its head and walked away in disgust to join the others.

8

Alan had settled himself on the settee after Alistair went to bed. He'd huddled in a warm ball in the sleeping bag reliving the events of the last few days as they drifted through his mind. He saw endless roads passing underneath him, sheep dogs, the sea, his home, bad feeling, noise, arguments. Then he turned his attention to the small warm living room. The fire still glowed comfortingly in the grate and the room was silent. So silent. Just a clock ticking somewhere. So silent. No cars. No noise. Silence. Pressing in his ears like cotton wool. Just the ticking of the clock on the mantelpiece and the light from the fire warming his face as he drifted and floated on the silence and fell away with the warmth of the room.

In the morning the light suddenly shining through the window interrupted his sleep as the curtains were drawn. He grimaced and folded his arms across his eyes. A voice came through the haze as he put his head in the sleeping bag.

"Come on son. Best be getting up now."

Alistair was somewhere in the room. Alan couldn't tell where. He was too busy protecting his face from the bright glare of the sunlight. He lifted his head and yawned widely. Then he sat upright with the sleeping bag hunched round his waist and rubbed his eyes with the palms of his hands. He opened them in a narrow slit until they became used to the light.

"Come on Alan," Alistair repeated, "we'll be late for the service."

Alan rubbed his eyes. He thought he'd heard correctly

but hoped that he hadn't. He looked at Alistair who was staring down at him and saw from the expression and the way he was neatly dressed that he was serious. Alistair was wearing his best grey suit. His face was shiny from a close wet shave and his grey hair was plastered down with Brylcreem.

"The what?"

"The Service. It's Sunday. Come on. Get yourself out of bed or we'll be late."

"I'm . . . agnostic," Alan said, yawning again.

Alistair stood looking down at Alan.

"Not in this house you're not."

Alan looked up at the strong old man.

"Do you mean it?"

"You know I do. I don't know how your parents have brought you up but if you want to stay here for a day or two you'd better get out of bed."

Alan stepped out of the sleeping bag. He pulled on his shirt and jeans as his brain reeled. A church! What next?

"You're not going looking like that surely?" Alistair said as he saw the faded jeans. Alan saw his escape.

"This is all I've got. I haven't got any decent clothes. It might be better if I didn't go eh?"

"Och nonsense, man. I've got a good suit you can borrow. I'll get it for you."

Alan sat back down in a state of disbelief and examined a hole in the knee of his jeans. When Alistair came back through he was holding up a coat hanger with a suit on it and a green tartan tie. The suit was so old it was almost fashionable.

"That'll fit you son. Get yourself ready now and I'll do you some toast if you want breakfast."

Alan could see from Alistair's expression that there was no turning back and he couldn't argue with the man who'd given him somewhere to stay.

"I'll er . . . I'll get ready then."

He cringed inwardly and walked to the bathroom. When he'd finished dressing he looked in the mirror at the unfamiliar figure staring back. The suit felt old in every way but it had a stately bearing about it as if even the material had captured some of Alistair's personality.

He tied the knot on the tartan tie several times looking in the mirror then finally turned away and did it success-fully free hand. The jacket fitted well even though it was a bit big across the shoulders, but the trousers were too long. He looked at them for a while and then hitched them up by the waist until they were the right length.

He looked at the bottom of the trousers as he moved his feet forwards and backwards trying to decide whether he looked ridiculous. He smiled as he saw his training shoes sticking out from underneath and then walked into the kitchen with his arms wide to present himself to Alistair.

"There you go," Alistair said with a smile, "I told you it'd fit. Are you having any breakfast?"

Alan sat at the kitchen table and buttered some toast while Alistair went out to put some tartan rugs over the sandy car seats. They drove off at a sedate speed along the main street, through the village. As they passed other villagers walking along the road, Alistair raised his fingers from the wheel in a slight wave and had the greeting returned.

They reached the end of the road, coasted slowly around the end cottages and followed it up away from the sea towards the croft. As they passed the croft Alistair cast a knowledgeable eye over his sheep and carried on up to the T-junction at the end of the road.

Alan had expected them to turn right towards Dalstrath but the car wheeled left heading the opposite way.

"Aren't we going to Dalstrath then?"

Alistair shook his head.

"I don't like that church Alan. Far too modern for my liking. I prefer the one at Portness."

As they drove, Alistair barely kept his eyes on the road. He was too busy looking at the other crofters' animals and land, gauging his own efforts against theirs. The car slowed at a field full of fat lambs.

"See MacKay's lambs?"

Alan looked, but by the way Alistair had asked the question, it was obvious that a reply wasn't expected. Alistair made a strange clucking noise with his tongue to show disapproval and then drove on.

Alan craned his neck to look back at the field. The lambs looked fine to him.

At frequent intervals the gaps in the fencing and gorse bushes revealed the view down to the sea. Alan had wanted to go along the beach the previous evening but had been so tired that he'd just stayed chatting to Alistair and finally fallen asleep on the settee.

Portness was the next village along the coast. It was bigger than Tiener but not a proper town like Dalstrath. The houses were larger than the ones in Tiener. The bell from the church clanged persistently as the local crofters gathered outside in the well kept graveyard.

Alistair parked the car and led the way as they joined the rest of the congregation waiting in the sunlit entrance to go into the church.

The church was more than a hundred years old and yet the orange sandstone it was built from looked clean and bright in the morning sunshine. Of course, there was no industrial grime to blacken its walls, only the salty sea wind smoothing its surface and tempering the curves.

Alan shuffled his feet, feeling self conscious among so many strangers. Some of the Tiener people nodded to him politely. It appeared that many people knew who he was already. News of a new face travelled fast in a village like Tiener.

They began filing into the church. It was dim inside and the smell of old books and wood polish hung heavily in the air. Bright sunlight from outside illuminated the stained glass windows and filled the nave with an awesome atmosphere. The blues and reds and emerald greens were as vivid as the day they had been set into their lead surrounds.

The pews were in short rows. Hard polished wood with no cushions. At intervals along the shelf in front of them were hymn books and bibles. Alan followed Alistair into the pew and sat down quickly. The high polish on the seat and the surprise of the hard surface made him slide sideways as he sat down.

The minister walked up the aisle and the congregation rose, leaving Alan staring up at them for a confused second before following their example.

"Good morning," the minister beamed.

He had a mild face with a shine to it like a freshly scrubbed schoolboy. Even his hands had a softness that contrasted with the ruddy complexions of the crofters attending the service.

"We will begin the service with hymn two one two."

Alan looked round to see what the procedure was. Alistair picked up a dull burgundy hymn book and nodded to Alan that he should do the same. Alan found the right page and cringed inwardly when he realized he didn't know the hymn.

He was totally unprepared for what came next. It took him so much by surprise that he nearly burst out laughing. Instead of the surge of a chord suddenly filling the air he became aware of a rasping noise. The church organ was a small harmonium and it was being played by an old lady wearing half moon glasses. She was squinting with great concentration at the music in front of her as her feet pedalled up and down on the manual pumps. The rest of the congregation were obviously used to the wheezing noise, but to Alan it sounded like an asthmatic old man.

The first chord of the organ faded slightly as the congregation began to sing until the lady pumped a little harder and the wheezing increased in volume. The minister launched himself into the hymn with great gusto but sang slightly behind everyone else. Meanwhile a woman in a large hat at the back of the congregation sang louder and more shrilly than anyone else. After several verses the hymn slowed and died. The congregation sat down without prompting and the minister climbed the pulpit.

Alan could feel his stomach muscles contracting with giggles. He wasn't sure whether it was nerves or embarrassment but the whole occasion was beginning to get to him.

The minister leaned his elbows on the brass rail, his face slightly raised as if trying to catch the rays from the stained glass windows. Then with one sudden movement he stared wide eyed at the congregation and his voice boomed out dramatically.

"Today I want to talk to you about the harvest. The harvesting of your lives. The harvesting of your souls." He smiled at the crofters in the front pew. "As ye sow, so ye shall reap."

Alan stared at the stained glass windows as the minister's voice rose and fell with a rhythmic lilt. The subject matter seemed to appeal to the crofters, but Alan found it hard to concentrate. He looked round the church, at the brass crucifix and the stained glass windows and the wood carving on the pulpit. At the foot of the pulpit was a country scene carved immaculately into the hard wood. He could see that one of the animals was a fox. Foxy. What had happened to him? He had seemed to be enjoying himself with Alan but then he had just shot off on his own. Where was he now? Maybe he was still in Dalstrath. He ought to go looking for him.

9

"You'd have thought he'd have phoned," Alan's mother said as she turned angrily from the television. "He must know we're worried sick. I mean, where's he got to stay? How do we know something hasn't happened to him?"

Alan's father ruffled the paper and stretched his legs out on the settee.

"He'll be all right. He's probably staying at a friend's house. But I'll give him what for when he gets home."

"I should hope you will. Four days now and not a word. How do we know he's not in hospital or something? How do we know that?"

"He'll be all right. He knows how to look after himself. He's probably sleeping on someone's floor or something."

Alan's mother stood up.

"For heaven's sake Ken. He's only sixteen . . . I'm going to call the police."

The evening paper ruffled noisily.

"Sit down! You know what Alan's like. He's probably just at a friend's house."

"Suppose something's happened to him? What sort of parents are we going to look like if . . ."

The telephone ringing in the corner of the room stopped her dead. They both stared at it, Alan's mother with her hand to her mouth. Alan's father threw down the paper.

"Well are you going to answer it or not!"

Alan's mother just stood there staring at the phone so he stood up and went to answer it. He picked up the receiver and sighed heavily.

"Yes."

A distant voice mumbled at the other end of the line.

"It's me. Alan."

"Alan! Where the hell have you been? Your mother's been worried stupid."

"I'm on holiday."

"What do you mean holiday? Where on holiday?"

"I'm at Uncle Alistair's."

"What!"

Alan's mother grabbed the phone.

"Alan. Where are you?"

"I'm at Alistair's."

"What on earth do you think you're doing going all the way up there? I've been worried sick."

Alan cleared his throat.

"I just had to get away. I was worried about . . ."

"You get yourself back here."

"I was just worried about jobs and . . ."

"Do you hear me?"

"I don't know what I'm going to . . ."

"Fancy running off like that. You're not in any trouble are you? Promise me you're not in any trouble."

Alan's voice began to crack as he tried to talk. To communicate. To explain.

"I'm just worried about what I'm going to do now that I've finished the exams."

Alan's father snatched the receiver.

"What's this about you being in trouble? If you're in any trouble you can pay your own fines. Our Kevin managed to stay out of trouble so I don't see why . . ."

The phone buzzed quietly as the line went dead.

Alan stood in the phone booth at the end of the dark main street. He breathed heavily and could feel the tightness in his chest. He could feel a numbness and a sense of turmoil in his guts.

He left the phone box and walked along the quiet street,

passing the dimly lit cottages and neat gardens. The few street lights in Tiener glowed brightly against the jet black sky. He could smell the seaweed and the fields and the cool expanse of sea behind the village as he walked back to Alistair's.

The warmth of the living room was welcome as he walked in and the smell of Alistair's pipe hung in the air. Alan looked at Alistair and gave a vague smile as the old man shuffled in his seat to see him better.

"You all right son?"

Alan nodded doubtfully. He sat down in the chair opposite Alistair and swallowed hard as he fought the inner turmoil.

"You all right Alan?"

The old man leaned forward in his chair, concerned at the look on Alan's face. Alan nodded yes, but his head just kept nodding, and nodding, and tears formed in his eyes and rolled down his cheeks. He rocked back and forth and the tears rolled on to his jeans leaving dark blue marks like the first spots of rain. He put both hands flat over his face and gave a cry for help from so deep inside him that it filled the room.

Like a dam breaking, all the hurt and torment came out. The lack of understanding. The sheer weight of existence without a purpose. He cried. He cried for the first time in years, through the hurt and the fear of a blank future.

Alistair rose from his chair and placed a hand on Alan's shoulder.

"So much to carry son."

Alan wiped a hand across his face.

"I'm all right."

Alistair said nothing. He just looked down, steady and sincere, as Alan spoke through his tears.

"I'm all right."

Alistair stood up and waited a moment.

"Do you want a dram?"

Alan nodded, so Alistair went to the sideboard and found a bottle of whisky and two glasses. He poured a good measure for both of them and then offered a glass to Alan.

Alan sipped the golden liquid, glad of the warmth that went through him as Alistair stood near.

"So Alan. What's wrong son? Trouble at home?"

Alan shook his head, both hands entwined round the small glass.

"I don't know. I'm sorry . . . I don't know."

The clock ticked. Alan put a hand to his face and drew it down his cheeks, easing the tension in his jaw.

"I don't know. It's like a tightness. Like . . . anger."

Alistair sat down in the worn chair and waited quietly.

Alan looked up.

"I'm sorry. I don't know what's happening to me. I can't explain. It just . . . sort of built up."

The tears began again in spite of Alan's attempts to stem them by smoothing his fingers across his cheek bones. He shook his head against the embarrassment of it.

"What's happening to me!"

Alistair looked on and took a drink from the whisky glass.

"You need a rest son. That's all. You need a rest."

"But what from?" Alan wiped his eyes angrily. "I'm sick of everything. You know what I mean? Just sick to the bones of everything."

Alistair waited, sensing him opening up.

"It just built up. The exams and everything . . . And this pressure all the time. All the time. Get a job. Do well . . . I didn't do anyone any harm or anything and it's just so . . . unjust. All this jobs thing."

Alan sighed, trying to put his feelings into words. Struggling with emotions.

"It's just . . . There were loads of chances for people my age once. It was all mapped out. And my parents haven't a clue. They say they care and that. But they haven't a clue how I feel. They don't listen to me. They just don't know how scary it all is. I've tried telling them but they don't listen."

Alistair lifted the bottle and poured them both another drink.

"You stay here Alan. For a few days. You don't have to go home. There's no hurry son."

"I don't want to go home."

"Aye well. You just take it canny now. A bit of work on the croft and a bit of good Scottish air will put a bit of spirit back into you. You'll see."

Alan sipped at the whisky.

"Thanks. I'll be all right." He looked up shyly. "Sorry."

Alistair smiled.

"Don't be son. No need."

10

There was a short blast on a car horn which made Alistair look up from his morning tea and glance out of the window on to the main street.

"That's Stewart for you now," Alistair said as he nodded towards the window.

"Right. I'm off then. See you around lunch time then," Alan said and made for the door.

Out on the main street Stewart's old car was billowing oily smoke. It revved noisily in the quiet of the village as Alan climbed in.

"Have you been to Dalstrath before then?" Stewart asked as they passed through the village and out towards the top road.

"Just when I came through it on the way here." Alan looked over the back seat at the interior of the car. "This yours then?"

Stewart laughed. "No. It's my Uncle's but he let me use it for the day. I can't afford my own car at the moment."

"You working?"

"No. I've just done 'A' levels. What about you?"

"I've just failed most of my exams and left school."

Stewart nodded. "What're you going to do now then?"

"I've no idea."

Stewart laughed. "Oh well. Being up here'll take your mind off it for a bit. There's the dipping tomorrow."

Alan frowned. "What dipping?"

"The lambs. We're sheep dipping tomorrow. It'll be all hands on deck. Mind Alistair will probably give you a few quid. Not that he can afford that much."

The car turned at the top of the village road and headed for Dalstrath.

"I thought you worked for Alistair," Alan said as he watched the seashore in the distance appearing at intervals through the gaps in the hedge.

"No. I just like helping out. I used to go up to the croft all the time when I was a kid and I just keep doing it. There's not that much to do in Tiener, so it passes the time."

"You used to come round when you were a kid?"

"Yes. Well for a good few years anyway."

Alan turned sideways in his seat and studied Stewart. There had been a freckled faced boy with red hair, he remembered. He burst out laughing.

"I remember you! You're the one with the stick!"

Stewart frowned. "What?"

"I was about five, so you'd be about seven. You always used to carry a stick. A broken shepherd's crook."

Stewart began to grin.

"Can you remember that?"

"Yeah. You used to wallop anything that came near and Alistair was always telling you off for poking the sheep or the dogs or anything else that you could hit."

Stewart laughed. "That's right, yeah." He glanced quickly at Alan and frowned, then turned back to the road. "You aren't 'Red Wellies' are you?"

"Yeah!"

Stewart looked in amazement at Alan and laughed loudly.

"Ha! It's old 'Red Wellies' himself."

The two of them laughed and kept looking at each other in amazement.

"Seems a long time ago now. Fancy remembering those red wellies," Alan said. "And now you're off to University. Who'd have thought it. The kid with the stick."

"I think there were a few people surprised about me taking 'A' levels. Not least me."

"I'd have thought you'd be a farmer."

"No. Not up here."

"Why not?"

Stewart shook his head and glanced either side of him as they entered Dalstrath with cars parked on either side of the main road.

"Too much like hard work."

He concentrated as he turned up a side street away from the main road and guided the car into a parking space in the public car park.

Alan climbed out and looked back into the front seat.

"I'll see you in half an hour then."

Stewart leaned over and called through the open door.

"Aye. I'll not be long. Just a few things to get."

Alan nodded and strolled off through the car park, down to the main street of the town as locals and holiday makers mingled on the narrow pavement, peering into shop windows.

The morning was grey. Rain threatened as the clouds hung heavily in the sky. Alan walked along the road with his hands thrust in his pockets. Half way along the main street he noticed steps leading off to a small public park. The gardens were neat and clean and in spite of the threat of rain the grass was parched and brown from the long dry spell. Rose beds were set out in pleasing shapes and brightly coloured blooms were at their best.

Alan came across a park bench and sat down, stretching his legs in front of him as he revelled in the quiet of the gardens. There were no other people there other than a young couple, walking arm in arm. They talked quietly to each other as they passed him. Then the girl laughed loudly at something the man had said and made to hit him playfully in a show of pretend anger.

Alan watched them leave as they climbed the small steps back up to the main street, then from the corner of his eye he saw a movement in the shadow of a bush. It was difficult to make out what it was from so far away so he walked across the grass to get a closer look.

When he was near enough he could see a pile of old newspapers, a black bin liner and the dull white shape of Foxy's sports bag.

"Foxy?"

A hand moved under the pile of papers and was still, listening, waiting.

"Now then. Foxy?"

The top paper moved and a pair of wild bloodshot eyes stared half focused as Alan moved forward a step.

Alan laughed loudly. "Foxy!"

Foxy stared and blinked, his face confused and uncomprehending.

"What's going on? What're you doing here man?"

"I came looking for you, idiot."

Foxy quickly scanned the gardens for any dangers and then sat upright, brushing the papers away from himself and combing his straggly hair away from his face with his fingers.

"Time is it?"

"About ten."

Foxy yawned widely. He slithered out of the sleeping bag and stood up, stretching himself.

"Got a smoke?"

"No. Do you want a cup of tea or something?"

Foxy's eyes flicked round the gardens as if the question were some sort of trap.

"Yeah. Right. Yeah."

"Come on you tramp. There's a coffee shop round the corner."

Foxy packed the sleeping bag and followed Alan as they

93

made their way through the gardens and into the small cafe on the corner of the main street. They bought coffee at the counter and sat at a table near the door of the steam filled room.

"So you didn't go too far then Foxy. It's good to see you."

Foxy gave a twisted smile.

"Yeah. I'm freezing man."

"You'll soon warm up. What've you been doing then?"

Foxy shrugged. "Just looking round. I was going to go back today. It's not much fun on your own."

Alan nodded. He was genuinely glad to see Foxy again.

"So how've you been living? What've you been eating?"

Foxy took a tab end from the ashtray.

"This and that."

"I can imagine."

Alan watched him as he lit the stub of the cigarette.

"I'll tell you what Foxy. Why don't you come back with me to Alistair's place? They're all really friendly."

"No," Foxy said and shook his head. "I don't want to stay at your relatives. It wouldn't be right."

"But why not? Alistair's a great bloke. He wouldn't mind." Alan watched as Foxy gazed into his coffee cup. "I tell you what Foxy. Maybe you could earn a few quid. It won't be much but it might help."

"How?"

"Alistair's going to dip the sheep tomorrow. I'll tell him I bumped into a friend of mine camping at Dalstrath, and you want to come up and help. Alistair'll give you a few quid if you help out."

Foxy cocked his head on one side and weighed up the information. His face looked pale and drawn and there were creases on his cheek from resting against the damp sleeping bag.

"What's this dipping then? I don't know anything about farm things and that."

Alan shrugged. "Me neither. But it's nothing special. They just fill this bath thing with liquid stuff for killing bugs and chuck the sheep in."

"Like a tank?"

"Something like that."

Foxy looked at the end of the cigarette and stubbed it out.

"So how high's this tank thing then? Only I don't know how heavy a sheep is."

"You don't lift 'em in Foxy! It's like a swimming bath. It's low. You just throw them in. And they scramble out the other side up a ramp."

"And this Alistair bloke might give us some money for helping?"

"Yeah, I think so. But it'll be a laugh anyway. You can stay at Alistair's and . . ."

"I don't want to stay at anyone's house man."

Alan looked at Foxy and shrugged.

"All right. All right. If that's what you want . . . Here. I'll draw you a map." Alan took a pen from his pocket and scribbled a map on a serviette. "That's where the croft is there, right. Just on the outskirts of the village. I'll tell Alistair about you. If you turn up tomorrow we'll be down by the shearing pens. All right?"

Foxy picked up the serviette and looked at it.

"All right. But I don't want to get mixed up in anything. I just want to earn a few quid."

"Fair enough," Alan said as he stood up from the table. "Anyway, I've got to go now. I'm getting a lift. Where are you going to sleep tonight?"

Foxy took another tab end from the ashtray and brushed off the ash with his finger.

"Don't worry about me man. I'll be all right."

95

Alan moved to the door. "Yeah well. Take care. And be there tomorrow."

Foxy lit the tab end and grinned.

"See you man."

11

Alistair had removed the sheet of corrugated iron that covered the dipping bath before Alan and Stewart arrived. He was busy filling it with clean water and the correct measure of dipping fluid as they climbed over the five bar gate at the end of the pens.

The dipping bath was set in the concrete floor of one of the exit channels from the shearing pens. It was one and a half metres deep and two and a half metres long with a sheer drop into the bath at one end from the pens. At the other end of it was a ramp, so that the sheep could stagger out into the drainage pen with its sloping concrete floor. The sheep had to be first driven down from the fields and into the pens and then lowered over the lip of the concrete floor into the bath.

"How's it going?"

Alistair looked up from stirring the murky liquid.

"Good morning boys. A fine day."

Alan leaned on the wooden railing and looked down into the bath.

"Smells strong."

"Och no. It'll do the trick. Mind you don't get any in your eyes though. It'll sting the eyeballs off you."

Alan straightened up. "It smells like it'll strip their wool off."

Alistair laughed and pushed his cap back on his head. "Not quite boy. Not quite." He looked up on to the top road. "Is that your friend Alan?"

Alan looked up and saw the distant shape of Foxy making his way down the narrow road towards the croft.

He was walking slowly and keeping close to the wire
fencing round the fields as if to hide himself from view.
One hand was clutching the white sports bag and the other
was thrust deep into the pocket of his leather jacket.

Alan raised a hand and shouted cheerily.

"Foxy!"

Even from that distance Alan could see Foxy's head dip
as if avoiding a punch. When he straightened up again he
extended a hand in a return wave and walked more
confidently towards the gate of the croft.

Alan ran down the side of the pens to meet him.

"You made it Foxy."

"All right Al. You working?"

"It's all O.K. I told Alistair you were on holiday and I
met you in Dalstrath. Just keep your ears and eyes open
and it'll be easy."

Foxy scanned the fields and the shearing pens, not
looking at Alan as he spoke.

"I've not done this before man."

"Don't worry Foxy. I haven't either. See that bloke there
with the ginger hair. That's Stewart. Just keep your eyes
on him. He knows how to go on. Come on. I'll introduce
you to Alistair."

Foxy climbed uneasily over the gate and followed Alan
towards the dipping bath. Alistair looked up as they came
near.

"Alistair. This is my mate Foxy."

Alistair put out his hand and smiled. Foxy looked at the
hand for a second before realizing he was supposed to
shake it.

"Oh yeah. Right. Hi."

"Pleased to meet you son. You on holiday are you?"

Foxy smiled nervously. "Yeah. Right."

Alistair stood upright and set his cap firmly on his head
as he looked out towards the sheep in the nearby field.

"Right then boys. I suppose we should get started now we're all here. I'll get the dogs. Stewart will tell you where to stand."

Stewart beckoned to Alan and Foxy to follow him as Alistair walked off.

"It's really simple. He's going to use the dogs to drive the sheep from that field there and bring them down here. All you've got to do is stop them going all over the yard and into the barn. If you stand here Foxy you can drive them into the pens."

Foxy swallowed nervously.

"They don't bite do they?"

"What?"

"The sheep. They don't bite do they?"

Stewart looked at Foxy to see if he was joking but noticed that he was serious.

"No. They won't bite. Just flap your arms a bit. Sheep are pretty stupid." He turned to Alan. "If you stand up there by the barn Alan, to stop them wandering off over there, that should about do it. When they get down to the pens come in behind them. O.K?"

Foxy and Alan nodded and Stewart walked further up the field towards the flock, leaving the two of them staring after him.

"You sure they don't bite man?"

"Give over Foxy. They're only sheep."

"Yeah well. They must eat with something."

"Just stand there. Leave your sports bag by the fence and when they come down past the pens flap your arms a bit and they'll go into that opening there. Once they start going they'll all go."

Foxy's head spun round quickly as Tam twanged the fence on the way to the sheep.

"I haven't done anything like this before, that's all."

"You'll enjoy it Foxy. Just watch these dogs. They're brilliant. I'm off up here. See you in a minute."

Alan left Foxy and walked further along the pens towards the yard and the open barn.

Foxy watched as Alistair expertly slipped between the third and fourth wires of the fence and followed Tam up the field. Rona, the smaller dog, bounded after Tam and then suddenly veered off at an angle and ran straight at Foxy. Foxy backed up against the shearing pen.

"Oh God!"

Rona scampered up to him and ran in a tight semicircle around him, barking and wagging her tail. She then stopped two metres in front of Foxy, and dipping her head, looked at him out of the corner of her eye. Foxy's eyes flickered nervously around the croft looking for help and his head automatically dipped and bobbed as it always did when he felt in danger.

Rona copied his movements and very slowly moved in on him, her haunches ruffled and her body low as if she had just discovered a strange looking sheep. Her tail wagged furiously as she slithered closer. Foxy realized he wasn't going to be mauled and he relaxed a little.

"What do you want man?"

Rona scittered backwards at the sound of his voice and barked loudly, excited by his voice and flickering eyes. Foxy suddenly noticed that the dog was almost copying him with its own nervous eye movements and he began to grin.

"All right dog? You working?"

He extended a hand to pat the dog, who flinched but slowly came nearer until Foxy could pat her on the head. Then Alistair's distant commands drifted on the wind and caught Rona's ears making them prick up. She was off like a bullet across the field to the sheep.

Foxy grinned and followed the dog's progress across the

field. Tam had already gathered the first hundred or so sheep into a loose flock and was driving them towards the yard. Foxy's eyes widened and he swallowed hard when he saw the mass of moving sheep coming towards him.

"Bleedin' hell! A stampede!"

The flock drifted slowly down the field and trickled uncertainly through the open yard, as Alan moved in front of the leading sheep and diverted them down the side of the shearing pens towards Foxy.

As the mass of sheep came closer, Foxy remembered something about flapping his arms. He began flapping them up and down like a demented bird man.

"Shoo you woolly gits! Shoo!"

The sheep at the front were so distracted by his movements that they stopped dead in front of him and then tried turning back into the on-coming flock. Finding no exit behind them and Foxy in front of them, they suddenly broke away and escaped round Foxy as he continued to wave his arms.

Alan saw Foxy flapping his arms and burst out laughing.

"Foxy! Foxy! Not so much! Now then Foxy! Not so much!"

Alistair began running down the field and shouted instructions to Tam, who ran through the fence and appeared behind Foxy, driving the sheep back towards him until Foxy was surrounded. He forgot his arm waving as he frantically staggered through the crowded sheep towards the safety of the shearing pens and climbed up on to the top of the wooden fencing.

Alan ran down the inside of the pens and climbed up on to the wooden fence with Foxy as the sheep filed past below.

"What're you trying to do Foxy?"

Foxy held tightly on to the wooden spars as the sheep moved past into the pens.

"They were after me man."

"They're only sheep."

"That's easy for you to say. I don't like the look of 'em."

Alan looked at the concern on Foxy's face and slapped him on the back. Foxy looked at him in surprise and then grinned. He looked at the sheep coming into the pens and then started laughing.

Alistair pushed the last of the sheep into the pens and laughed as he passed Foxy.

"You looked like you were having trouble taking off son."

Foxy shuffled uncomfortably on the fence.

"It's all a bit new to me this, see."

Alistair smiled and walked towards the dipping bath.

"You're doing fine son. Don't you worry."

Stewart came up to them and pulled a packet of cigarettes from his jacket pocket. He offered one to Foxy.

"Best have a break now before all the excitement starts. Once Alistair gets going you won't be able to stop him."

Foxy took the offered cigarette and looked uneasily at the sheep crowded into the pens.

"What happens now then?"

Stewart pointed up to the pen nearest the bath.

"We want to be up there next. I'll show you how to go on."

Foxy and Alan followed Stewart up the side of the pens to where Alistair was getting ready. As they walked, Alan turned to Foxy.

"Fancy yourself as a shepherd Foxy?"

Foxy tried to look offended but couldn't help smiling.

"Not every day you're terrorized by four hundred lamb chops is it man?"

12

Alistair put on a bright yellow sea fisherman's cape and lowered himself into the hole next to the dipping bath. It was a small concrete hole in the ground. When Alistair stood in it his waist came to ground level and he could lean over and push the sheep under the dipping fluid with the flat of his hands.

He gave the grey liquid one more stir with an old sweeping brush and looked up at Stewart.

"All right boy. Here we go."

Stewart stubbed out his cigarette and climbed over the fencing into the pen nearest the tank. He kneed the crowded sheep out of the way and opened a small gate in the fence so that the only exit for the sheep was into the bath. They shuffled nervously and tried to keep away from the opening.

Stewart leaned across the top of the nearest sheep and wound his right hand across its chest to grab the left front leg. His left arm tucked underneath the other side of the sheep, then he stood up lifting both its front legs off the floor. He began shuffling backwards heaving the confused sheep with him towards the gap in the fence. He wrestled it until it backed through the opening. As Alistair guided it over the lip of the concrete floor, he let it go.

There was a huge splash as the sheep tumbled completely over on to its back and disappeared beneath the murky dipping fluid. It surfaced and bucked until it was the right way up again, blinking against the stinging liquid and struggling to get out of the bath. Alistair pushed it under the liquid again with the flat of his hands holding it down for the required length of time. When he was satisfied that it was fully soaked he let it go. It struggled like a drowned rat to the concrete ramp at the end of the bath and scrambled out shaking itself and bleating pitifully as it galloped into the corner of the drainage pen with its sloping concrete floor.

Stewart grabbed another sheep. It struggled against him to try and stop itself going into the bath but he had a firm hold of it and shuffled it towards the opening. He heaved its rump over the concrete edge and let it go into the bath. Alistair held the sheep under the water again before releasing it to join its companion.

Foxy and Alan peered over the fence.

"Is he trying to drown 'em or what?"

"They've got to be done properly Foxy."

"Yeah, but even then. He holds them down such a long time."

"It's regulations."

Alan turned back to the dipping bath as Stewart called to him.

"Come on Red Wellies. Do you want a go?"

Foxy looked at Alan in astonishment.

"Red who?"

"Nothing."

"He said Red Wellies."

"Forget it."

Stewart grabbed another sheep and manoeuvred it into the dipping bath.

"Come on. I'm not going to do it all by myself."

Foxy took a backwards step and looked nervously at Alan.

"You have a go man. I'll watch for a bit."

Alan climbed over the fence into the pen and struggled through the sheep until he reached Stewart. He watched the next sheep go over the lip of the bath and then grabbed hold of the nearest one with both hands round its neck. It bucked and pulled out of his hands as he spun round trying to keep hold of it. Stewart called over to him.

"No. No. Like this."

He grabbed a sheep over its shoulder and grasped its front legs as it bucked and skidded on the hard floor. He moved one hand to grasp it round its middle and then lifted its front legs completely off the ground. He then walked backwards, pulling the sheep with him until he could lower it over the lip of the bath.

Alan scratched his chin and looked at Foxy. Foxy was grinning from ear to ear as he watched.

"You can laugh Foxy," Alan shouted. "It's your turn next."

Alan rubbed his hands together and grabbed the nearest sheep. He managed to get a firm hold on to its wool and heave it towards the bath. After a mighty push the sheep did a belly flop into the bath and sent a spray of the eye stinging liquid up into the air.

Alistair ducked back as the spray nearly hit him.

"Steady now boys! Steady!"

Stewart pushed the next sheep towards Alan.

"You're getting the idea, but they're supposed to go in backwards. You're supposed to lower them in. Grab them over the shoulder and lift them. That way they can't do anything about it."

With Stewart's guidance Alan managed to dip another sheep successfully. He shouted across to Foxy.

"Come on Foxy. It's a good laugh this."

"In a minute."

"Come on. They won't bite you know."

Foxy sighed uncertainly and climbed slowly on to the fencing. He watched for a few moments and then stepped down into the crowded pen.

"Which one do you want then?"

Stewart looked up as he grabbed the next sheep.

"Take your pick Foxy. They've all got to be dipped."

Foxy looked round the bleating flock and picked a small lamb that was pinned in a corner by a few of the larger ones. He waded towards it and tried to grab it but he couldn't get it out of the corner for the press of the others in the way.

"Take one over here Foxy. Don't drag it all the way from over there. Get an easy one."

Foxy licked his lips and went nearer the bath. Then he lunged forward and grabbed a sheep by the rump with both hands. It scrambled across the concrete floor with Foxy holding on to it, his training shoes skidding across the hard surface.

"Grab its neck Foxy!" Alan shouted after him. "Turn it round. Grab it by the legs over the top."

The sheep that Foxy had hold of stepped backwards suddenly and placed a hoof squarely on his foot. He let out a yelp and pulled his foot sharply out of the way.

"Right!" he shouted. "That's it pal. I'm mad now!"

Even Alistair laughed as Foxy angrily grabbed the sheep around its middle and lifted its front legs off the ground. He grunted and shuffled it backwards until he came to the gap in the fence, then Alistair grabbed the lower half of the sheep and guided it into the bath. It fell over on to its back and disappeared under the dipping fluid.

"That showed it Foxy," Alan laughed.

Foxy smiled.

"He knew not to mess with me man."

"She. It's a her."

"Whatever," Foxy said as he lunged at the next sheep.

They were at it for an hour, then Alistair stopped them and filled the bath to the right level again while Stewart let the dipped sheep back into the field and herded the sheep from the back pens into the dipping pen.

Foxy took off his jacket and rolled up his sleeves as he began to enjoy his work. He'd watched Stewart carefully and now had the technique off to a fine art.

"Better than practising judo this is," Foxy said as he swiftly immobilized the next sheep and shuffled it towards the dipping bath.

"Och yes," Stewart said dryly. "It'll stand you in good stead if you ever come across a sheep with a machete."

Foxy nodded and lowered the sheep into the bath.

"Don't get many of those around our way. Not recently anyhow."

Several hours later, when all the sheep were done, Foxy and Stewart sat on the ground next to the pens and lit cigarettes. Alan sat on the fence and wiped the sweat from his forehead as the three of them panted with exhaustion.

"Is it always like that?" Alan asked.

Stewart looked up over his shoulder.

"Yeah. But it doesn't happen that often so it's not too bad."

Foxy looked at the burning cigarette and blew a satisfying cloud of smoke into the air.

"I'm shattered man, but that's the best fun I've had in years."

"See I told you," Alan said as he flexed his arms to ease the ache in his shoulders.

Foxy looked up at Alan and shrugged.

"Yeah. Well. I didn't know chucking sheep around was fun did I?"

Alistair came back from the sheds minus his bright yellow protective clothing and walked up to them.

"Well I think a cup of tea and a bite to eat would be a fine thing. Are you boys coming down with me?"

Foxy looked up at Alan.

"Yeah, why not," Foxy said quickly. "I could kill a cup of tea."

Alan smiled and climbed down from the fence.

"Yeah. Great."

They drove in Alistair's estate car back to the village dropping Stewart off on the way. When the dogs had been seen to, Foxy and Alan went into the living room and collapsed on the settee while Alistair put the kettle on.

By the time Alistair came back through with the cups of tea, Foxy was sprawled out on the settee with his mouth wide open, snoring peacefully. Alan was slumped next to him with his eyes shut.

Alistair smiled when he saw Foxy. "I see hard work agrees with your friend there."

Alan opened his eyes and looked across to Foxy, asleep next to him.

"I don't think we're used to hard work. Not that sort anyway."

Alistair sat down in the battered arm chair by the fire.

"There's not a lot of room, but your friend's welcome to sleep on the floor tonight if he likes."

Alan looked at Foxy and then back to Alistair.

"Well. I was going to tell you really but . . . well Foxy doesn't like staying in other people's houses. I don't know why, but he doesn't. We came up here together but as soon as we got to Tiener he shot off and went to Dalstrath on his own."

Alistair took a sip of his tea and licked his lips slowly.

"I suppose the two of you could camp up at the croft if you like," he said and leaned back in the chair. "You could put your tent up behind the sheds."

Alan scratched his ear.

"Er, well. You see, he hasn't actually got a tent. I just said he was camping because . . . well it sounded better."

Alistair raised an eyebrow and took another sip of his tea. He thought for a moment and then came to a decision.

"The two of you can stay in the back shed at the croft if

you like. You could treat it like a sort of chalet if you gave it a bit of a sweep. There's nothing much in there mind, but you could make yourselves comfortable without too much trouble. It's dry and warm at this time of year."

Alan looked up surprised.

"Yeah?"

"If you want to that is. You'd be with your friend there, and it'd be no bother to me just so long as you leave the things on the croft and don't meddle with anything. You could come down here for a bite to eat in the mornings."

"That'd be brilliant!"

Foxy heard the raised voice and suddenly woke up. He blinked a few times and sat up on the settee with a startled look.

"What? You what?"

"Oh, you're back in the land of the living."

Foxy rubbed his face and got his bearings then reached out for his cup of tea.

"I must have been asleep man."

"Get away?"

"It's tiring slinging sheep around. And this sea air really does you in."

"Now then Foxy," Alan said eagerly. "Alistair says we can stay in one of the sheds at the croft. Like a chalet."

"Yeah?"

"Not so quick," Alistair said hastily. "It's only a shed with windows but I thought you'd prefer it to being all squeezed in here."

Foxy nodded enthusiastically.

"Sounds all right to me man."

"All right then," Alistair said. "When we've had something to eat I'll take you up there and you can have a look."

13

The "chalet" shed was as Alistair had claimed. It was just a small shed behind the main row of sheds on the croft and it had a couple of windows on either side. Inside, it was dry and musty but once the few bags of fertilizer had been moved and the pitchforks cleared out of the way, there was enough room for the two of them to make themselves comfortable. Tucked in a corner were two trestles and a couple of planks so Foxy immediately made them into a bed and claimed it as his own.

"Look at that man," Foxy said as he dumped his sports bag on the wobbly structure. "I've even got a bed."

Alan looked at it critically as he continued sweeping the floor.

"You can't sleep on that."

"Why not?"

"It won't take your weight."

"Rubbish," Foxy said and showed how much rubbish it was by pushing at the planks with the flat of his hand. "Better than a hotel bed that."

Alistair poked his head round the door and looked in at them.

"How's it going boys? Will you be all right here?"

"Yeah, great."

"I found you a paraffin lamp. You shouldn't be too cold but you'll be needing a little light." He shook the lamp to check that it had fuel inside, then placed it on a small shelf behind the door. "Go careful with it now and only use it in here."

"Thanks a lot," Alan said cheerfully. "It's as good as a holiday camp this."

Alistair laughed. "Well I don't know about that. I'd prefer it if you slept down at the house but I know you want a bit of freedom, so if you're comfortable, then you're welcome."

"No, this is great," Alan said quickly. "Thanks a lot."

Alistair smiled and felt in the pocket of his coarse woollen trousers. He produced three five pound notes and pulled off two.

"There you go boys. That's for helping me out with the dipping. I'm just going to do a few jobs now and then we'll go down to the house. All right?"

Foxy took the offered note and smiled broadly.

"That's brill. We even get paid for chucking sheep about."

Alistair laughed. "Oh don't worry boy. You'll earn your keep by the time you leave." He then dipped his head through the door and disappeared up the field.

"He's a good bloke isn't he?" Foxy said as he sat on his makeshift bed.

"Yeah," Alan nodded. "It was good of him to let us use this shed. I told him you didn't want to stay at the house so he came up with this idea."

Foxy frowned. "What did you tell him that for?"

"Well it's true isn't it? It was you that said you didn't want to stay at someone's house."

"Yeah, well ... It sounds rude though. You needn't have told him that. I could have gone off to Dalstrath again."

"Oh yeah? And sleep in a plastic bag somewhere?"

"Well," Foxy shuffled uncomfortably. "You shouldn't have said I didn't want to stay. It sounds bad man."

Alan raised his eyebrows.

"Don't blame me! I just told him what you said.

111

Anyway, why don't you want to stay at the house? We could have slept on the floor easily enough."

Foxy shrugged. "I just don't like staying in someone's house. It doesn't feel right."

"Probably frightened you'll nick something," Alan said jokingly.

An angry expression crossed Foxy's face.

"Don't ever say that Al! That's not funny! I just don't feel comfortable right! That's not funny that Al!"

Alan held his hands up.

"All right. It was just a joke. Sorry."

"It's not funny that man."

"All right. Sorry."

"Just because you had a nice home and everything doesn't mean everyone else did. My Dad didn't like anyone coming back. I never had anyone back at our place because he used to give them such a bad time. And he used to play hell if I went round someone's house for tea. 'Your own home not good enough?' he used to say. Only 'cos he was on the dole and ashamed about it because everyone else seemed to be right well off."

"Yeah, all right. I'm sorry."

"It gets to you after a bit Al. It got so I felt guilty going to someone else's house. Always wondering if me Dad would find out. That's what it's all about. My Dad used to play hell because he thought it meant he wasn't good enough."

Alan leaned against the door frame. He could feel his face reddening with embarrassment at his own stupidity. He smiled weakly as Foxy sat silently on the bench bed.

"A weak spot me thinks."

Foxy looked up and realized Alan was repeating his comment about Alan's girlfriend. He smiled and kicked a stray piece of straw on the floor.

"Yeah, well."

Alan laughed and broke the silence.

"Well that's two subjects we know not to talk about."

"Yeah."

They sat quietly for a second then Foxy grinned.

"Now then Al. You been to the beach yet?"

Alan shook his head.

"Not really. I went down to the shore the other night for a look but I've not been along the beach properly."

"Right," Foxy said loudly. "We'll go beach crawling when we've finished here."

"Do what?"

"Beach crawling. Looking for stuff. You know."

Alan raised his eyes to the ceiling.

"Beach combing! It's called beach combing."

Foxy shrugged. "Whatever."

After they'd been down to Alistair's house they set off through the village towards the beach. As they walked past the small cottages various people smiled at them or wished them a good day. They returned the greetings or smiled back.

"Weird," Foxy said quietly as they passed another person who'd greeted them with a friendly smile.

"What is?"

"Everybody's dead friendly. Like they know us."

Alan shrugged. "It's only a small place. I bet everyone knows exactly who we are and where we're staying."

"Really?"

"Yeah. You'd be the same if you saw the same people day after day."

"Bit weird though," Foxy said thoughtfully. "It's like being famous. I could walk into town from our house a million times and no-one would say hello."

When they reached the end of the houses they cut through a sandy field and across to the shore. A light breeze caught them as they went over the rise and down to the beach. Foxy whooped with unrestrained joy and ran down on to the sand like a five year old on his first holiday.

"Look at this man. There's nobody here!"

Alan caught up with him and looked up and down the gravelly beach that stretched round the village. There was no-one in sight in either direction.

"Where is everyone?" Foxy said as he kicked at a bit of seaweed and made a cheering noise in the back of his throat to show that he'd just scored a goal.

"They'll be working or something Foxy."

Foxy picked up a long dangling piece of seaweed and sniffed it, then he swung it several times round his head and tossed it towards the sea fifty metres away. It left his arm and flopped to the ground just in front of him.

"Rather them than me man. This is brilliant. I think the sea's brilliant. Can you smell that Al? Just smell at the air man."

Alan stopped and frowned as he sniffed the air.

"I can't smell anything."

"No. Look. Just smell."

Alan sniffed the air again.

"I can smell the sea."

"Yeah," Foxy said excitedly. "Brilliant, eh?"

Alan watched Foxy and then smiled. He had taken off his shoes and socks and was running at full speed towards the tiny waves at the edge of the sea. Alan laughed and ran down after him as he splashed in and out of the water.

"Beats living in a crummy city any day this Al," Foxy said as he took a swipe at a wave with his foot. A spray of water flew into the air and then blew back towards him as the breeze caught it. He grimaced and spat and then carried on walking up the beach on the fringe of the waves.

"It's brilliant this Al. I'm right glad I came. That Alistair's a really nice bloke letting us stay in that shed

114

thing. I don't feel like I give a monkey's about anything just now. It's great."

Alan picked up a flat pebble and skimmed it on the water. It bobbed two times and then disappeared beneath the waves.

"Yeah. It feels like we should stay here and forget going back."

Foxy spun round. "Yeah! Let's stay here. Stuff jobs and college and all that stuff. I think I'll just stay here dipping sheep and that. Better than staying with our Terry in the flat any day."

Alan picked up a piece of drift wood and dragged it in the sand as he walked. It carved a satisfying groove behind him and threw up a small furrow of sand like a plough.

"You know what really gets me," Alan said as they walked. "It seems like we've been gone for ages. Know what I mean?"

"Yeah," Foxy said. "It's only Tuesday now and it seems like we've been gone weeks."

"I'm really glad I came."

"So anyway," Foxy said as he dried his feet on the back of his jeans and began putting on his socks. "What was up with you anyway? I mean I'm glad we shot off and everything, but you weren't right when we left."

Alan frowned and stopped walking.

"What do you mean, not right?"

"Well you weren't were you? You looked like you were cracking up or something when I met you in town."

"Yeah well," Alan said and started walking again. "I'd just had a bust up with my parents."

"Oh, yeah. I know that one. My dad used to play hell with me all the time."

"So I just thought I'd get lost for a bit that's all."

"Don't they know where you are then?"

Alan shrugged and turned away.

115

"I phoned them. They just shouted down the phone at me."

Foxy nodded. "Our Terry wouldn't care where I was. Nobody would, come to think of it."

Foxy squinted further up the sand towards the fields and then ran off up to the tide mark with its cluster of dried seaweed and tin cans and rubbish. He began kicking at the debris as he walked and then stooped to pick up an old petrol can. He shook it a few times and then tried to get the screw top off it but it wouldn't budge, so he ran back down to the sea with it and lobbed it over arm into the waves.

"What did you do that for Foxy? Mucking up the sea."

"Give over man. That's where it came from. Anyway the tide's coming in. It'll get washed up again."

Alan watched some sea foam swirling in a thin stream of water.

"The tide's going out."

"Rubbish."

"It is."

Foxy pointed to another wave as it cascaded back up the sand.

"What's that then?"

"It's coming in now but . . ." Alan pointed as the wave went back down the beach. "There!"

"Rubbish!"

"It's going out Foxy!"

"It's a wave. It's got to come in and out but it's coming in more than it's going out. Anyone can see that."

"Bet you."

"It is!"

"Bet you!"

"Right then."

"To that mark there."

Alan pulled the stick across the point the wave had last

reached and made a mark in the sand, then the two of them watched like two professional gamblers waiting for the results of a horse race. The next wave broke and sent a thin wall of water up the beach like a puddle from a spilt bucket. It soaked into the sand as it went and stopped just short of the line.

"There!"

"That was a freak wave that man. No energy. It were just pretending to go out that's all."

The next wave slewed up the sand and just wiped out the edge of the mark.

"There! See!" Foxy said excitedly and stood right over the part of the mark that had been touched by the water as he pointed his finger. "There see! It touched!"

"It's going out!"

"Balls!"

"It is then!"

They watched in silence as the next wave came up the beach. It fell very short of the line.

"See!"

Foxy stood up and scowled.

"It's the seventh wave that comes in. We've got to wait seven waves to see which way it's going."

"Oh yeah?"

"Yeah. I saw it somewhere. Papillon. That's it. It was this film, right? About a French convict called Steve McQueen. He fills this sack full of coconut husks and lobs himself off a cliff."

Alan looked at Foxy and burst out laughing.

"He does what!"

"It's true. This Papillon bloke wants to escape from a prison island. So he fills this sack full of coconuts and chucks himself off a cliff."

"Neat plan."

"It was."

"There!" Alan pointed to the wave as it now came very short of the mark and drifted back down the beach. "That is definitely going out!"

Foxy looked critically at the line and then watched the next wave come in. It fell short and drifted out again.

"Yeah well," Foxy said as he shrugged.

"Yeah well," Alan mimicked walking further along the beach. "And where do you think all that water came from anyway," he went on pointing to all the small pools that had been left from the recent tide.

Foxy scowled and followed on behind.

"Yeah well. It might have soaked up through the sand while it was coming in."

Alan smirked. "Go jump off a cliff."

"Let's just find some coconuts first," Foxy said as he scuffed his training shoes in the sand.

They walked a little further up the beach and then cut back through the fields and headed towards the village. Foxy fell back as they walked, poking at tufts of grass with his foot or looking at some small insect that had caught his attention. Eventually Foxy lost sight of Alan as he disappeared ahead over the hump of a grassy sand dune.

Foxy walked through the spiky tufts of grass, down into a hollow and then stopped as the sound of the sea was muffled behind the dunes. He moved his head sideways slightly like someone listening to a distant sound, then put a finger in his ear and shook it like someone going through a tunnel and feeling the pressure on his ears.

He yawned and did slight chewing motions, trying to clear the stuffed up feeling in his ears, then he put his head on one side again like a timid bird, listening.

Then he realized and laughed out loud. It was the sound of silence.

There was nothing. Nothing to hear. The village was far away. The sea was over the sand dunes. For the first time in his life he was aware of silence. No cars. No voices. No doors slamming. No conversation or juke box or radio. No television. Nothing.

He clapped his hands just to see if they still made a noise. Then he laughed and said "ah, ah, ah", fascinated by sound in this peaceful place.

"What're you doing Foxy?"

Foxy looked up and saw Alan staring at him from the top of a sand dune.

"Now then Al. Come down here a minute."

Alan skidded down the sand dune into the dip and walked over to Foxy.

"What? What is it?"

"Listen."

Alan stood still and listened with widened eyes. He looked at Foxy and then listened again.

"I can't hear anything."

"At all?"

Alan listened again.

"No."

Foxy smiled.

"Isn't it brill."

14

The first thing they heard as the dim dawn light began filtering in through the window of the shed was the noise from the rooster. It was the second morning in the shed so they knew what to expect but were no more used to it than the first time they'd been woken up.

Foxy turned over and made himself comfortable on the planks as a sheep bleated in the distance. Then the rooster crowed again and Alan shuffled inside his sleeping bag and pulled the quilt up to his ears. A seagull called a few times and another sheep bleated. The rooster crowed once more and the hens in the shed nearby began shuffling and clearing their throats in a quiet murmur of early morning activity.

"Oh ... Not again," Foxy mumbled and pulled his sleeping bag over his head.

The sound of the sheep grew louder until the whole flock seemed to be bleating to prevent Foxy getting back to sleep. Then a seagull landed on the roof of the shed and scratched out a path across the hard surface as it pecked at the tarpaulin. A cow mooed somewhere in another field.

Alan mumbled and turned over on the floor, then peered with startled eyes over the edge of the sleeping bag at the shed window. The light coming in was barely visible but it was obvious from the noise of the farm animals that dawn had arrived. He put his hands over his head, snuggled down into the sleeping bag and drifted in a semi-stupor.

Foxy shuffled a few times and then also drifted back into sleep as his tiredness overcame the strange noises.

A while later the two of them were wide awake, lying in

the warmth of their sleeping bags and debating whether to move or stay where they were.

"Did you hear that rooster again this morning?" Alan asked as Foxy's eyes peered at him from the sleeping bag.

"Yeah," Foxy said grumpily. "I could quite happily string the thing up." Foxy sat up with his sleeping bag bundled round his waist. "Shall we get up then?"

"What time is it?"

Foxy looked at his watch and grimaced.

"Half seven."

"Half seven!"

"Yeah."

Alan sighed heavily and sat up from the floor.

"I'm not going to sleep any more I suppose."

"Let's get some breakfast eh?"

"Yeah."

They set off down through the village and were greeted by the smell of fresh toast as they entered Alistair's house. Alistair had been up and about for two hours by the time they arrived and had just sat down for his morning tea.

He looked up and smiled cheerily as he flicked the page of his newspaper.

"Good morning boys. Fine day. Did you sleep any better this morning?"

Foxy rubbed his gritty eyes and shrugged.

"I'd like to strangle that rooster."

Alistair laughed and went through to the small kitchen with them.

"Have yourself some breakfast boys. Then I've a wee job for you."

Foxy and Alan argued over the last piece of toast and then they went up to the croft with Alistair in the estate car. Alistair led the way to one of the sheds and ducked his head as he went inside. Leaning against the wall was a large sledge hammer and a metal spike two metres long.

121

"I've got to put some posts in boys," Alistair explained as he handed the hammer to Foxy and the metal spike to Alan. Carrying the tools they followed Alistair through the fields and out to the land on the perimeter of the croft.

At the edge of the field was a border of uncut grass that marked the original position of the fence before it had been taken down. The old fence posts with broken ends lay at intervals along the ground together with the new fence posts.

Alistair placed his hand on Alan's shoulder and pointed down the length of the field.

"Now there you see boys. The new posts are on the ground at the places I want them. And the bottom wire is already on the strainers here." He turned slightly sideways to indicate what looked like a sawn off telegraph pole sticking out of the ground where the gate would be. "That's one strainer and the other is that one you can see at the end of the wire." He nodded across the line of the fence to another large pole sticking out of the ground. "All you have to do is follow the line of the wire and put the posts in where I left them. I'll do one or two to show you how to go on."

He took the spike from Alan and positioned it carefully in line with the wire. He then lifted the spike a few centimetres and thrust it into the ground. Its weight and its pointed end made it stick in the ground quite easily. Alistair moved it steadily back and forth to widen the hole.

"That's just the starter, see," he explained. "Now we just take a post and hammer it into the hole."

He took one of the new wooden fence posts and placed its point into the narrow hole made by the spike. Alan held it upright as Alistair swung with the hammer and drove the new post into the ground.

They worked their way down the line of the wire with Alistair hammering and Alan or Foxy holding the posts, until they had done four more, then Alistair laid down the hammer.

"There you go boys. Not much to that really. Can you do that? I've got a few other jobs to do now."

Alan and Foxy nodded. They watched Alistair as he smiled and walked back down the field with the air of someone at peace with the world. Alistair seemed to have a softness of tread and steady pace that was in rhythm with the land.

"I'll do the hammering," Foxy said and grabbed the hammer before Alan could protest.

"Well just watch my fingers that's all."

"Me?"

"Yes you."

Alan walked down the fence to where the next fence post should be placed, dug the metal spike into the ground and began prising it back and forth. When he'd finished he placed a new wooden post in the hole and held it upright.

Foxy lifted the hammer at full arm's length and was about to swing at the post while Alan held on to it, but Alan took one look at the angle of swing and let go. The hammer skidded off the side of the wood.

"Foxy! What're you trying to do!"

"You let go man!"

"You nearly had my bloody hand off!"

"Rubbish!"

"You did! Hold the hammer further up the handle for God's sake."

Foxy picked up the hammer with a firm grip. He then nodded at the post.

"Well are you going to hold it or what?"

"Just watch what you're doing that's all."

"I know what I'm doing man. I know about hammers. You can't tell me about hammers."

Foxy tapped the post lightly a few times to make it firm,

then raised the hammer high over his head. Alan flinched and stepped backwards letting go again.

"What's the matter with you?"

"You'd have had my flaming hand off."

"It wouldn't have missed."

"You're not trying to win a prize at a bloody fair Foxy!" Alan held the post upright again. "Just tap it a few times right. Tap it so that it stands up on its own. Then you can knock hell out of it if you want, but not while I'm holding it."

Foxy tapped the top of the post gently. Eventually the post stuck upright and Alan let go and stepped back, so he swung his arms up over his head and gave it an almighty bang with the full weight of the hammer. The post went deep into the ground perfectly upright.

"Look at that," Foxy beamed. "I've won a coconut."

"Good," Alan said. "A few more and you can shove them in a sack and chuck yourself off a cliff."

Foxy looked at Alan and started laughing. He lifted the hammer up and carried on banging the post down into the ground as Alan went to the next post and began making the hole with the metal spike.

"You know what Al?" Foxy said between hammer strokes.

"What?"

"If you'd have told me last week I'd be standing in a field in Scotland putting up a fence of my own accord, I'd have thought you were mental."

Alan grinned. "Yeah. It's daft isn't it."

"I'm enjoying it an' all. That's even more stupid. My dad used to try all sorts of things to get me to do stuff and then go mad because I wouldn't. And here I am putting up a bloke's fence, just for fun. I must be going barmy."

"Didn't you get on with your Dad at all then?"

Foxy shrugged and stopped hammering.

"Well . . . My Dad was always rowing with my Mum. And then we used to cop it when he was feeling mad . . . Too many Uncles man."

"You what?"

Foxy looked at Alan and shuffled self consciously.

"You know . . . 'Uncles' . . . My Mum was always messing around with someone. I used to come home from school when I was skiving off or something. When I was young . . . and she used to look all flustered. 'This is Uncle Pete' she used to say. Or 'Uncle Tom' or whatever and then get me out of the house by giving me money for sweets . . . It was years before I twigged what was happening." The hammer rested on the floor as Foxy continued. "Then my Dad found out and he hit the roof. He was rotten after that to all of us. Terry got it worse than me. He used to really hit Terry. We had the Social and the police and all that round."

"Was that when you were at school then?"

"Yeah. Fourth year. Then Terry got a flat and I went with him to get out of the way. Terry can be a bit of a mean git but he's not as bad as my Dad. He could knock seven bells out of anyone, my Dad. He was a Hammer Driver before he got the push."

Alan began pulling back and forth on the metal stake. He felt uncomfortable hearing about Foxy's home life.

"What's a Hammer Driver then?"

Foxy started banging the wooden post again as he spoke.

"A Hammer Driver. You know. He's the one that presses the button to make the press come down. You know . . . that huge hammer in the steel works. They bash massive lumps of steel with it . . . I went once with me Dad and he showed me. There were bits of metal there as big as a bus and red hot. You could feel the hair on your face singeing when you were miles away from it . . . Responsible job that, Hammer Driver. If you get the timing wrong you can kill someone easy as spit . . . Then he got the push and he went a bit funny. Sitting around at home all day."

Alan didn't say anything. He couldn't think of anything to say.

"But anyway," Foxy continued. "I'm well out of all that lot now. Nothing like getting away to give you a bit of breathing space eh?"

Alan nodded. "I'm still aching from that sheep dipping though."

"Yeah, me too. That was good that," Foxy said. "Gets rid of all your aggression, chucking sheep about."

"You think so?"

Foxy walked over to Alan and picked up the next fence post.

"Yeah. You've only got to look at Alistair. No tension there man. Because he spends all day beating up sheep."

Alan laughed and moved out of the way as Foxy placed the fence post in the hole.

"I feel better now than when we set off."

"You didn't look very happy."

"Yeah, well. It's all this exams thing."

"You too?"

"What?"

"Wondering what you're going to do?"

"I suppose so."

Foxy picked up the hammer and looked at Alan.

"You're like me."

Alan frowned and began walking to where the next hole should be.

"Since when have I ever been like you?"

"You are. Same as the rest of us. We're all piddling about like something with no head."

"Speak for yourself."

"I am man."

"How do you mean?"

Foxy rested his elbow on the hammer and looked back at the croft sheds. He seemed to have forgotten what he was going to say for a moment and then nodded to himself as if he'd just found the thought.

"Nobody knows what they're doing anymore. That's what I'm saying. Not anyone. That's it."

"What's it?"

"Well ... My Dad, right. He's been made redundant two times. Twice in a year. And most of the time he doesn't give a monkeys about me or anything. Especially me. But it's no wonder when you come down to it ... How can you go on if you don't know what's round the corner eh? That's what gets me. How can you plan something if you don't know what you're going to be doing in a month? Eh?"

"I suppose so."

Foxy scratched his head and looked at the grass.

"I mean, you don't know what you're going to do with yourself over the next year. I don't. My Dad doesn't. So who does eh?"

Alan frowned and began digging the spike into the ground.

"That's a bit deep that."

Foxy looked at Alan in astonishment and laughed.

"Me! Deep! That's good that is."

"Well you don't half come out with some stuff sometimes. I thought you were supposed to be stupid the way you put yourself down and that."

Foxy frowned. "I'm not stupid man. No-one is. You just don't get asked the right questions."

Foxy shrugged and began hammering the fence post into place, then he put the hammer down again and rested on it.

"Listen. Right ... Everybody's lousy at something. I bet Einstein were rubbish at football."

Alan removed the spike and put the next post into the hole.

"If you're that sharp why do you keep going round nicking things?"

"Who keeps going round nicking things?"

"You do."

"Yeah, well."

"So why do you keep nicking things if you're that clever?"

"Because they're there man. I never took anything off anyone. Not off real people. It's just from cig machines and stuff. I never picked anyone's pocket or anything. When did I ever nick anyone's savings then?"

"I don't know . . . Did you?"

"Oh come on man. I'm not that bad. You know I'm not that bad."

"Well I don't know do I?"

Foxy looked at Alan critically and realized that he wasn't joking.

"I just take what's there. Everyone takes what's there. It's what it's about. If it's there you grab it. Nobody ever gave me anything. So if it's there, I have it."

Alan said nothing. He waited for Foxy to finish hammering the wooden post.

Foxy looked at him a few times and seemed embarrassed by the silence. Eventually he lowered the hammer again and looked at Alan.

"I'm not that bad man."

"Who said you were?"

"You did."

"When?"

"Just now."

"I didn't."

"You might as well have. I don't nick anything you

128

know. I just take it. I take what's there. If it's there I take it."

"Oh very cute. Look great in court that will."

"Leave off man."

"All right. Forget it."

Foxy came across to where Alan was standing, holding the wooden post.

"Mind your hand."

"What?"

"Shift your hand or you'll be a thumb missing."

Alan looked at his hand on the fence post and moved it smartly out of the way as Foxy lifted the hammer. He paused with the hammer in the air and looked at Alan.

"I'm not that bad man."

15

It was early evening and Alan and Stewart were already astride the bicycles as Foxy strode down the main street of the village to Stewart's house. He walked up to them and looked at the bicycle Alan was sitting on.

"That's neat man. How come we can't use Stewart's car to go to Dalstrath?"

"I can't get it tonight," Stewart said as he tapped the pedal with his foot. "Anyway Dalstrath isn't that far."

"And you're sure they'll let us into the pub then?"

"Aye, you'll be all right if you're with me. You both look about eighteen anyway."

Foxy looked at Alan and saw him trying to hide a grin.

"What you laughing at man?"

"Nothing Foxy. Nothing."

Foxy frowned and looked around him. "So where's my bike then?" Alan snorted down his nose and turned away as Foxy looked at him. "Am I supposed to walk or what?"

Stewart smiled and freewheeled his bike a little forward. Behind it was a bicycle resting against the garden fence. Foxy looked at it and turned to Stewart as Alan began laughing.

"I can't ride that!"

"Of course you can," Alan said. "There's nothing wrong with it."

Foxy looked at the bike propped against the fence. It was a monster of black metal.

"It's an antique!"

"It's all right," Stewart said as he turned his bike to see Foxy better. "It works anyway."

The bike was an angular construction painted matt black. It had a chain guard and full mud guards and sit up and beg handle bars. On the front was a small wire frame basket for holding shopping.

"Desperate Dan's got a smaller bike than that man!" Foxy said as he pointed at the bike accusingly. "It looks like something for bashing castle doors in with. Are you sure your mother doesn't use it for ploughing or something?"

Stewart laughed. "She uses it now and then. It's the only one I could borrow. Come on. No-one cares about things like that round here."

Alan began moving off to prompt Foxy, but he was still staring at the black monstrosity as if it might bite him.

"People might see me."

"Nobody cares. Come on."

Foxy reluctantly pulled the heavy bike away from the fence and sized it up. He turned the handle bars left and right a few times as if he expected them to come off in his hands.

"You sure people don't care about this sort of thing?"

"Don't be daft."

Alan and Stewart set off up the street on their modern bikes leaving Foxy to wobble unsteadily behind them. He drifted uncertainly back and forth across the road as the handle bars wavered in his hands and then caught up with them.

By the time they'd cycled up the slight incline away from Tiener and on to the top road, Foxy's legs were beginning to ache in places he'd forgotten existed.

"You all right?" Alan called over his shoulder.

"Oh just brill," Foxy said breathlessly. "Considering I'm driving a tank I'm doing great."

"It's not that bad," Stewart said. "Anyway it gets easier now. There's a long down hill stretch from here."

"Good job," Foxy said quietly.

As they pedalled down the slight slope along the top road to Dalstrath Foxy found that he was actually enjoying himself. Even if he was driving Desperate Dan's bike. If he'd been back home he wouldn't have dared be seen on the thing, but so far away in Tiener he didn't feel so inhibited.

He smiled slightly as the breeze ruffled his hair and Alan and Stewart streaked off in front of him. It had been years since he'd been on a bike. He leaned forward and pedalled harder until he eventually caught up with them.

"What's that crop over there?" Alan asked, pointing to a field at the side of the road.

"That's just grass. It's hay," Stewart said.

Alan looked round at the countryside and could see outlying crofts and the patchwork of different colours in the fields. In one field were sheep with a blue mark on their wool just above the shoulder.

"What's that funny mark?"

"Funny what?"

"The blue marks."

Stewart looked to where Alan was pointing.

"Oh. That's like a brand. It's just dye so that they can be identified in case they get out or mixed with someone else's sheep."

Foxy sat up in the saddle to peer over the hedge as they passed the field. The bike veered dangerously across the road so he quickly sat down and heaved the handle bars straight.

"I never saw that before," Foxy said. "What's Alistair's mark then?"

"A red spot. On the neck."

Foxy laughed and lifted his feet off the pedals.

"He ought to call the croft 'The Old Red Spot Corral'. You know. Like they do in cowboy films. You could have a shoot out in Tiener. Red Spot Corral versus the Cow Pat Ranch."

Alan looked over his shoulder as the clanking of Foxy's bike came up behind him.

"How you doing Foxy?"

"Oh, you know," Foxy said as he grinned and began singing. "Old man Foxy . . . Dat old man Foxy . . . He just keep rolling along."

The three of them were laughing as they entered the outskirts of Dalstrath and headed towards the Claymore pub. Outside they propped their bikes against the wall and chained them up, then walked together towards the pub. Foxy, thinking he was dealing with things he knew, took the lead towards the door. Then Stewart called to him.

"Not that bit Foxy."

Foxy looked at the door and then back to Stewart.

"I thought we were off in here?"

"Yes, but not that bit."

"What's wrong with it?"

"We want to keep a low profile. That's the smoke room."

Foxy and Alan looked at each other and followed Stewart into the lounge.

The lounge bar was peaceful. A handful of people were talking quietly in the corners of the room, but there was no juke box or crowds of people as Alan and Foxy had expected.

"What do you want then?" Stewart asked as he pointed them towards a table.

"A pint of lager," Foxy said eagerly.

"Me too."

From their seat, Alan could see across the bar to the Smoke room. It was a small room with a dart board and tiled floor. Only five people were in there. All men, either in farm clothes or scruffy overalls and at least three of the five were stupefied with the effects of whisky and were swearing fluently in guttural Scottish accents.

Stewart came back with the drinks and sat down.

"See why we didn't go in there now. You'd have stuck out like a sore thumb."

They all took a sip of their drinks and stared round the room.

"So what're you going to do with your 'A' levels then?" Alan asked.

Stewart licked his top lip and put the glass down.

"I'm off to Edinburgh hopefully. Engineering."

"Sounds interesting."

Stewart shrugged. "It's just an excuse to get away from Tiener really."

Foxy frowned and looked at Stewart over his glass.

"What do you want to get away for? It seems great to me. No rush. The seaside. Even the people are friendly."

"It's not as simple as that."

"What then?"

Stewart picked his words carefully.

"You don't see it the same coming from a big city, but there's nothing up here for people my age. Not now anyway. That's why everyone's moving out to do something else. Going to University or something."

"What's wrong with working on a farm then?" Foxy asked. He turned to Alan for support. "That's what I'd do man. Who needs engineering rubbish when you can work on a farm?"

"That's the problem though," Stewart continued. "There isn't enough land available now to make a living. Well you can but it's really hard work for what you get. That's why Alistair's sons moved off to Canada. Running a croft is hard. So they took off to Canada."

Foxy took a swig of his lager and wiped his mouth thoughtfully.

134

"Sounds daft to me. I'd stay in Tiener."

"Me too," Alan added.

Stewart smiled knowingly and nodded.

"You don't see it the same. Tiener's a really small village. If you lived there you'd understand. Everyone knows everyone else. They're all living in each other's pockets. And once you've been to all the places nearby there's nothing to do." Stewart lowered his voice slightly. "You see those people over there?"

Foxy and Alan looked across the lounge bar to where Stewart had nodded.

"Yeah."

"Well. I know every one of them. Not really to speak to. But I know who they are and where they live. I even know who they're related to. I bet you don't get that where you come from."

Foxy laughed. "Hardly."

Just then, two girls came into the pub. One had curly brown hair and was wearing a short light blue skirt. The friend who was following her had on a T-shirt with Bruce Springsteen written on it. She flicked back her fair hair as she walked across the room and smiled at Stewart.

Foxy looked at Stewart and then back to the two girls as he spoke out of the corner of his mouth.

"I reckon you've cracked it there man."

Stewart looked at Foxy.

"What?"

"Those birds. I reckon they're giving you the eye."

Stewart glanced at the girls and then laughed.

"I've been out with them already."

"Yeah? Which one?"

"Both of them."

Alan and Foxy exchanged grins and leaned forward.

"What? Both at the same time?" Alan asked.

"No. Don't be daft. I mean over a period of time."

Foxy chuckled to himself.

"You get about a bit don't you?"

"It's not that. Have a think about it," Stewart said. "There's only so many people the right age. It's not like being somewhere where there's thousands of girls the same age as you like you've got in a city. You end up meeting them all sooner or later."

"Yeah. I never thought of that," Foxy said. "It must be a right bind bumping into ex-girlfriends all the time."

Stewart shrugged. "You get used to it. If you stay here long enough you end up marrying the girl next door. Literally."

"So what do you think you'll get out of leaving then?" Alan asked. "Besides a larger choice of women that is."

"Oh I don't know," Stewart said almost flippantly. "It doesn't matter. It'd just be great to get away. To live a little. You've come from a big city and think it's great round here because it's different, but it isn't when you get to know it. It's a dead end place."

Foxy twiddled the empty beer glass in his fingers as he watched the froth settle in the bottom.

"You've depressed me now."

"Sorry." Stewart took the glasses. "Another one then?"

"I'll get them," Alan offered.

"No, I'd better go to the bar. They might ask your age. Give me some money when I get back."

When Stewart had left the table Foxy looked across at Alan.

"He must be mad man. It's great round here."

Alan shrugged. "I don't know. Maybe it's like he was saying. There's nothing for anyone our age round here."

Foxy looked across the bar and leered at the two girls. "Oh, I don't know."

"He's right though," Alan continued. "There can't be

that much going on really. I mean there can't be a lot of opportunities."

"No," Foxy said as he pulled his thoughts back to the conversation. "He wants to try living in our town for a bit. That'd get him straightened up."

When Stewart came back from the bar the conversation drifted on to other things. The pub filled up as the evening progressed but not to the proportions Alan and Foxy had expected. The drinks started to go to their heads and they laughed loudly as people came and went in the small bar. Stewart nodded occasionally to acknowledge someone he knew, but said little as Alan and Foxy chatted.

By the time they went outside for the bikes their faces were slightly flushed from the laughing and drinks. The street lights were on and the dark sky above them was jet black and sprinkled with stars. Foxy heaved the black bike from against the lamp post.

"Now hold on a minute. I've got to get this tank into gear. I don't want to go in reverse down the main street."

Alan and Stewart grinned as they mounted their own bikes and pulled away. The two of them cycled off in front of Foxy as he pedalled after them with exaggerated effort.

"Hold it! I think the anchor's dragging or something."

Stewart shouted back at Foxy.

"My mother rides it without any trouble."

Foxy could be heard laughing behind them.

"And a fine body of a woman she is too. What does she do for a living. Prop Forward?"

"I'll tell her you said that."

"Don't do that," Foxy said quickly. "I don't want to mess with anyone who can ride this thing."

Alan and Stewart stopped for a moment to put on the lights on their bikes and then set off again as Foxy began to catch up with them.

"Hey!" Foxy shouted. "Where's the lights on this thing!"

Stewart called back to him. "There aren't any. There's not much traffic here anyway."

"Oh brill," Foxy murmured. "What happens when we run out of street lights?"

The last of the street lights was already visible as they approached the edge of the town.

"Just follow us. You'll be all right."

As they progressed away from the street lights along the dark road, Foxy felt increasingly nervous as he followed the two red lights in front of him.

"You still there Al?"

"'Course I am."

"Good," Foxy said quietly. "I thought I might be following a UFO."

They cycled for a while in the darkness until they were well out on the top road in the countryside. Then the silence was punctuated by a crash of a bike and swearing.

"Oh no!" Stewart said half laughing. "I forgot to tell him about the ditch."

"The what?" Alan asked.

"The drainage ditch down the side of the road. Didn't you see it coming in?"

"No."

They turned their bikes round and went back to where the noise was coming from.

"Hell fire! I think I've broke me leg!"

"Where are you Foxy?"

"I'm here man!"

Alan and Stewart cycled to the lump of black metal and pointed their front lights into the ditch. Alan wanted to sympathize but seeing that Foxy wasn't hurt he couldn't help laughing. Foxy was lying in the ditch with the bike on top of him.

"Get me out of this hole man!"

Stewart put his bike down and began trying to prise Foxy's foot back through the spokes of the wheel.

"Will you leave me alone!"

"I'm only trying to help."

"Well don't try and help."

"I'm just trying to push your foot back. There. Done it."

Foxy stood up and heaved the bike out of the ditch then brushed himself down.

"That's a neat trick that is. Digging a hole where you don't expect it."

"I should have told you," Stewart said apologetically.

"Yeah, you should."

"Anyway," Alan said. "You should have been right behind us."

Foxy sat back on the bike and pushed off as he followed the other two.

"I was behind you. I hit a bump."

Stewart looked behind him. "There aren't any bumps on this road."

There was a moment's silence then Foxy's quiet voice could be heard just behind them.

"Well there must be a depressed hedgehog somewhere."

16

The morning was bright and the windy day had blown away the clouds, leaving the sky clear as the coolness of the sea breeze eased its way across the barley and hay, swaying it smoothly in waves of changing colour.

Alistair looked at the distant fields, at the crops and the sheep, at the barley and the hay almost ready for cutting, and smiled with pleasure. The tractor had seen better days and the sheds were worn from their years of service in the hard Scottish weather, but he thought of how the croft had been when he was a small boy and felt proud of his accomplishments.

The barn had only been put up in the last ten years. Its solid structure had been built with good timber and the labour of anyone who would help. The farm machinery was not the most modern, but the best he had been able to afford. It pleased him to see the army of machines in the yard, built up in his lifetime.

He thought of his two sons and how he missed them. Canada was so far away. So far from Tiener. But he knew that they were doing what was right for them. They were laying out the future for other generations as his own grandfather and father had done. It was just sad that their futures were in another country, away from the heritage of crofting. There was no-one to carry on now. No-one to build on his efforts and take them to a further stage. A further generation.

So many things had changed in his lifetime. He remembered as a boy how he'd had to go to the village well to get water. It made him smile now, to think how it had been.

The village well was boarded up now and hadn't been used for years. But as a boy it had been his job, every morning, to go to the well with two huge buckets and get enough water for the day. When he came back from school he would do the same trip again.

Then pipes had been laid and the whole village transformed in just two years. Running water! In every house! No more going to the well. Just turn on a tap and there you go.

It had been the same with electricity. He remembered the upheaval and protests and confusion of all the roads being dug up and the old folk swearing that they wouldn't change their ways, but being carried along with the times in spite of their protests.

And the village telephone. Alistair laughed as he remembered. The red phone box at the end of the main street had caused more excitement than men landing on the moon. A telephone box! In Tiener! The gossip and conversations for weeks were about the phone. Who you'd be able to phone. How much it cost. And the endless conversations in the pub where everyone discussed in scientific detail the procedure for making a phone call.

The only way of making a phone call before the telephone box had been installed was from the village Post Office. And that could only be used when the Post Office was open. This inconvenience was added to by the fact that the Post Office was also the village shop, so if anyone made a call the whole shop would go quiet, eager for gossip and entertainment at the caller's expense.

Kenny MacKay had been the first to use the phone box. He'd hung around for days while the box was being installed, asking the engineer questions. How to phone Australia. How to get your money back if it didn't work. Then he had found out when it would be working and waited for three hours outside the box until the engineer

141

said he could try it. By that time there had been quite a gathering around the box.

People had peered through the windows as Kenny dialled the operator. "What number do you require?" Kenny had flushed pink and fumbled for a ragged piece of paper in his jacket pocket. He had shouted the number so loudly that everyone outside could hear. "That will cost 2d caller." Kenny had pushed the two old pennies into the slot. The dialling tone sounded. Great excitement. Kenny had shushed everyone as he edged into the corner of the box and pressed the phone hard to his ear. "You're through caller. Please press button A." He had pressed the button and shouted as loud as he could at the only person he knew who had a phone.

Alistair grinned as he was brought back to the present. So many changes in his life. All the time things were changing.

He looked up to the top field where Alan and Foxy and Stewart were working on the new fence. They were fine boys. Stewart was always helping here and there, not out of any duty but just because he enjoyed the land and the work involved. Maybe that's where the future of the croft lay. The young could take the changes. They knew how to adapt and move with the times.

He saw Alan and Foxy laughing at something and wondered at what crisis had driven them to Tiener. Alan's problems he could understand. He knew that Alan was having difficulties at home. He had lived in Elaine and Kevin's shadow too long. It would make anyone seek the peace of Tiener. And though he was well removed from Alan's situation, Alistair could understand his need to find a place in society for himself, to know for what work or career he was destined. Everyone went through that. Everyone. For some it was a painless transition from boyhood to manhood with a way already dictated to them by parents or destiny. But for others there was a void of worry and confusion until they saw their true vocation. Alan would find what he was looking for. Eventually.

And the Foxy character. There was a strange one. So shifty in the way he moved. The way his eyes flitted here and there, like a haunted man. Like a wanted man, always looking over his shoulder. But he'd done nothing to make Alistair think of him as a dishonest person. In fact there was a childishness about him that was quite genuine. He couldn't hide his real self under the disguise of being confident. He was exactly what he appeared to be, a young man with many undiscovered abilities, haunted by a lack of confidence. He was all right, Foxy.

Alistair turned from the gate and walked to the car. The two dogs yelped and thrashed their tails as he sat in the seat and started the engine.

Up in the field the tractor engine also kicked into life as Stewart put it into gear and moved it a few more metres down the line of the fence. On the back of the tractor was an iron bar with the drum of wire threaded across it. As Stewart drove, the drum revolved releasing the wire, ready to be tacked to the fence. When he had let out sufficient wire Stewart stopped the tractor and climbed down to join Foxy and Alan.

Foxy picked up the staples and carried on where he'd left off.

"Now then Al," he said as he began tapping the wire into place. "How long do you think this fence will be here then?"

Alan shrugged. "I don't know. Ask Stewart."

"Now then Stewart . . ." Foxy began.

"I'm not really sure. It depends on how good the wood is. Fifteen years maybe."

"What?"

"Well something like that."

Foxy whistled, impressed.

"That's nearly as old as me that. I'll be over thirty by the time this comes down again. Imagine that man. I'll be over thirty. That's almost an old age pensioner," Foxy said and continued with his stapling. "Now then Stewart. Do you ever go fishing?"

Stewart looked across. "No not really. The tide goes out too far. You'd need a boat really."

"Shame that. I fancied a go at that."

"We could go flukey fishing this afternoon if you want. The tide's right out at three."

"Do what?"

"Flukey fishing."

Foxy lowered the hammer. "I thought you just said you can't go fishing round here without a boat." His eyes widened. "Have you got a boat?"

Stewart shook his head. "No. It's not like fishing with a line. You do it with your feet."

Foxy and Alan looked at each other and Foxy burst out laughing.

"You do what?"

Stewart grinned, realizing that they wouldn't believe him.

"There's small channels that run down to the sea. Down along the shore towards Dalstrath. When the tide goes out you can sometimes find stranded fish in the deep pools. Small flat fish. Flounders. Like plaice. Those are the ones you catch with your feet."

Alan and Foxy looked at each other and then back to Stewart as he sat on the grass grinning at them. Alan's hammer hung limply at his side as he studied Stewart's face.

"He's winding us up Foxy."

"It's true," Stewart said. "Honestly. Flukey's just a local name for flounder. And you catch them with your feet."

Foxy laughed. "How's that then? Do you kick 'em to death or what?" .

"No, no. If you want to have a go I'll show you."

Foxy nodded. "This, I've got to see."

"It's a joke Foxy. He's just kidding us on," Alan said as he went back to his stapling.

"I'm not kidding," Stewart said. "I'll show you this afternoon when the tide's right out."

17

Alan and Foxy trudged behind Stewart as he lead the way along the beach towards the small estuaries which cut up through the land. The sun had come out and was shining brightly when they finally reached the place they were heading for.

"This is the best pool up here," Stewart said as he pointed to a small trickle of water coming from a wide sandy based stream. "The big pools are further up."

Foxy and Alan followed as they walked up the sandy banks and followed the line of the wide stream. As they walked, the sandy bottom of the water became darker and deeper, and at intervals there were large pools, left by the retreat of the tide.

"We'll try here," Stewart said and sat on the bank to roll up his trouser legs.

"What're we looking for?" Foxy said as he also removed his shoes and socks and rolled up his jeans to his knees.

"You'll soon find out."

Alan hovered at the edge of the water and stared critically into the dark pools.

"I still think this is a joke Foxy."

"Give over man. Got to be worth a try this. I've never caught a fish with my feet before. Aren't you coming in then?"

Alan looked awkward and walked a bit further up the bank.

"I don't like things round my feet. Not things I don't know about anyway."

"Foxy," Stewart called. "Just follow right behind me and you'll see what I do."

Foxy nodded as the two of them strode into the water. The sandy bottom of the pool was light and clearly visible as the small puffs of sand flowed up under their feet and drifted down behind them. Stewart walked slowly with his head down, looking at the sand below him as Foxy followed in his footsteps.

"If this is a joke man . . ."

"Just watch Foxy. Just watch."

They walked another metre, slowly and carefully and then Stewart suddenly pointed.

"There!"

"Where!"

"There!"

Foxy looked but could only see the same clear sandy bottom where Stewart had pointed.

"Didn't you see it?"

Foxy frowned. "See what?"

"A fish."

"Nope."

Alan grinned from the side of the pool.

"He's having you on Foxy."

Stewart took another few careful steps forward and then pointed. A shape flew at speed from near his toes and zig-zagged across the bottom of the pool It was a small flat fish about the size of an outstretched hand. It moved a metre away and then just disappeared from view.

"Yeah!" Foxy shouted. "What was that!"

"That's a flukey," Stewart said simply. "That's what we're looking for."

"Where did it go?"

"That's what you've got to watch."

"Hey Al," Foxy shouted. "This is brill man. I just saw a fish."

"Very good Foxy."

Foxy followed Stewart closely as they moved forward. Then another pale brown shape suddenly took flight and skirted away in front of them.

"Did you see that?"

"Yeah. Where'd it go?"

"There. Watch."

Even Alan was beginning to show interest as they crept forward. He'd seen the shape too.

Stewart trod carefully as the stream of water moved round his knees. He walked to a spot a metre forward and stopped as he pointed at the sandy surface rippling below them.

"See it?"

Foxy moved round Stewart very slowly and stared at the point Stewart was showing him.

"No."

"There."

Foxy stared. "What am I looking for?"

"See its eyes there. It's buried itself in the sand. That's its eye sticking out of the sand there."

"Yeah?"

Stewart held his arm out to stop Foxy coming any closer.

"Watch."

He lifted his foot in the water and very gently lowered it over the place he'd been pointing to. He froze about two centimetres above the sand and then suddenly stabbed his foot down and stood on the ground hard.

"Got it!"

Foxy lowered his face right to the water but couldn't see anything for the cloud of sand billowing from the stamped foot. He looked up at Stewart accusingly but was stopped by Stewart holding his finger up to silence him.

"I haven't told you the next bit yet."

"Oh yeah?"

"When you pick them up, you do it by sticking your finger in their gills."

"Give over man!"

"It's true!" Stewart said.

"I haven't seen the fish yet," Foxy said and peered into the water at Stewart's foot, "never mind shoving your finger in its gills."

"Just watch."

Stewart very slowly crouched and dipped his body as his right hand went down the back of his calf to his right ankle. He paused for a second, feeling round his feet and then seemed to be grasping in the sand with his fingers. He found where the fish's head was and poked his middle finger into its gills. Then he suddenly stood upright waving the flapping fish in the air and heaved it towards Alan, who watched with amazement as it flopped beside him on the grassy bank.

The fish was wide and flat with fins that ran down the side of its saucer shaped body. On its belly side it was dark white and on the top side, were the two eyes and brown speckled skin.

"Wow!" Foxy shouted. "It's real!" He bounded out of the water and stood over the thrashing flat fish. "Look at that Al! He wasn't kidding!" Foxy poked the fish with his finger as it shuddered up and down the grass. "Look at that man. A real fish!"

"See," Stewart grinned. "I wasn't kidding."

Foxy bounded off into the water sending clouds of sand into the stream.

"I've got to have a go at this man. This is great."

"Don't stamp about Foxy!" Stewart shouted. "Just walk quietly. They'll move off and you'll see them if you just do it slowly."

Foxy nodded as his eyes went wide searching the sand.

149

He walked slowly one way and then back again and suddenly shouted as a fish shot out from under him.

"I saw it! I saw one. Where'd it go?"

Stewart came back into the water and went over to him.

"You've got to follow them with your eyes. See where they bury themselves. Let's walk up here a bit."

The two of them walked a bit further up the stream and then Foxy pointed.

"I saw it. There." He very carefully walked towards the shape he'd seen disappear in the sand and stood over it. "Damn. Where's it gone?"

Stewart was behind him and pointed at the sand. "There."

Foxy stared harder and could just see the vague shape of the fish beneath the sand. "Oh yeah."

He took a timid step forward and raised his foot over the ripple in the sand, then just as he brought his foot down the fish shot off behind him.

"You little git!" Foxy shouted after it. "I'm coming to get you."

He followed the trail in the sand and saw the fish ruffle its fins and slowly disappear beneath the surface like some strange hovercraft. He walked gently towards it and raised his foot very slowly over the shape. His foot suddenly pushed down and he held it tight to the ground.

"Yah! I got one! I got one Al!"

"Pick it up," Stewart said. "Find out where its head is and stick your finger right into its gills. But don't lift your foot up or it'll get away."

"Yeuch," Foxy said. "It feels just like standing on a wet fish with no socks on."

"It would."

"And I'm supposed to stick me finger in its ear am I?"

"Its gills."

"Yeah well. It's disgusting either way."

150

Foxy chuckled excitedly to himself and felt round the side of his foot until he could work out where the fish's head was.

"Hold it tight now," Stewart warned. "It's slippy."

Foxy bit his bottom lip thoughtfully and slid his middle finger over the body trying to find the gills. He shivered and laughed nervously.

"Oh that feels horrible. Oh dear . . . oh dear that is . . . oooh."

His face suddenly set with determination as he forced himself to overcome his squeamishness and thrust his finger into the gills of the fish. He let out a short yelp of disgust and then stood up triumphantly, waving the fish on the end of his finger.

"Look at that! A fish! I caught a fish with my foot! Look at that!"

He ran out of the water and let the struggling fish slip from his fingers as he stood over it and watched.

"Look at that Al. You have a go. It's amazing."

Alan pulled a face and stood up.

"No. Not me. You have another go."

"What's up?"

"I just don't like things tickling my feet that's all."

"It's dead easy man. Honest."

Foxy bounded back into the water and walked near Stewart as Alan reluctantly took off his shoes and socks and rolled up his trousers. He joined them, looking nervously at his feet as he walked in the water.

"There!" Foxy shouted excitedly. "See that Al?"

Alan flinched and looked up as Foxy pointed at an invisible shape somewhere in front of him.

"There Al. See it?"

"No."

"Here. Come here."

Alan moved up stream until he came to where Foxy was

standing like a pointer dog aiming his finger at the sandy floor of the stream.

"There. Just stick your foot down there."

"Me?"

"Yeah. Go on. It's dead easy."

"You do it."

"I've done it already. You have a go."

Alan saw where Foxy pointed and took another step nearer. He raised his foot and lowered it carefully over the fish, then stabbed down hard.

"Oh God!" Alan cringed. "That feels horrible."

"Grab it!" Foxy shouted excitedly. "Grab the little bleeder! Stick your finger in its ear 'ole!"

Alan began to reach down to his foot, but he wasn't standing on the fish firmly and just as he began to bend, the fish fluttered its fins and tickled him in the instep of his foot.

"Jeeeezaaaargh!!!"

Alan suddenly bolted backwards and ran for the shore in a spray of water as if being chased by piranhas. His knees kicked high in the air and his arms flailed as he scrambled for the bank. Then he rubbed his feet up and down on the grass and shook himself as a shiver went the length of his body.

"Oh God! That was horrible!" Alan shouted. "That was the most disgusting thing I've ever felt."

Foxy began laughing and then saw a fish heading straight towards his bare toes. The panic set up by Alan suddenly affected him and he lurched backwards, kicked his legs out of the water and launched himself at the bank.

He scrambled out of the water and sat down, scratching an imaginary itch from the sole of his foot.

"You've got me at it now Al. I was all right till you did that."

"It's horrible," Alan said again as a shiver went through him. "Like standing on wet liver."

Foxy felt for the cigarettes in his jacket and lit one as he stretched out on the bank grinning to himself.

"Nobody back home will believe us."

"It's not surprising."

Foxy looked over at the two fish on the bank and poked them with his finger. He let a thin stream of smoke escape down his nose as he shouted to Stewart.

"Do you reckon we can eat 'em?"

Stewart looked up from the stream and laughed.

"There's not enough there to feed a sparrow."

"I'm going to cook 'em man. We'll build a fire eh?"

"Give over Foxy," Alan said as he looked over his shoulder at the two small fish. "You wouldn't know where to start."

Foxy took another thoughtful drag of his cigarette.

"It's easy man. I've seen it on TV. You just put 'em on a stick and cook them over a fire until they look horrible. We just need a few more."

Foxy flipped the end of the cigarette and put the tab in his packet, then stood up.

"O.K. fish," he said decisively, "I'm coming in."

18

Foxy turned over restlessly on the hard bench in the shed and squinted over towards Alan. Alan was lying on the floor huddled in the warmth of his sleeping bag and appeared to be sleeping.

"Now then Al?"

Alan stirred but didn't reply.

"Al?"

There was a rustle as the body in the sleeping bag turned towards Foxy. A pair of half closed eyes peered at him in the semi-darkness.

"What?"

Foxy leaned up on one elbow and looked down at Alan.

"Do you think I'm evil?"

"What?"

"Do you think I'm evil. Am I an evil sort of person?"

Alan groaned with the effort of having to think and rubbed his face with his curled up fists like a rabbit on an Easter morning, then huddled deeper in the sleeping bag.

"What are you talking about?"

"I've been thinking," Foxy said. "I've been thinking. And I thought of all the people that said I was no good. You know what I mean? All those people. Teachers and my parents and people and that. They think I'm a bad person. I'm not a bad person Al."

Alan sighed heavily and adjusted himself to a more comfortable position as he half opened his eyes.

"Who said you were evil?"

"Everybody."

"You don't want to listen to everybody. What does everybody know anyway?"

"Yeah," Foxy said. "That's what I've been thinking. I'm not evil. Not really."

"Good. Now go to sleep. It's Sunday tomorrow."

"What's Sunday got to do with anything?"

"Nothing."

"And so I thought about it, right," Foxy continued in a half whisper. "I thought . . . What if someone had told me I was good at something? No-one ever said I was good at something, so I never was. See what I mean?"

A muffled grunt answered the question so Foxy took it that he was being understood and carried on.

"So I think that it's not really my fault. Well it is my fault but it's only my fault because I didn't realize that it was other people telling me I was bad all the time. You get to thinking that way after a bit. If you tell someone something they start to believe it. And . . . everyone told me I was bad. So I did bad things all the time because that's what I thought I was like . . . And it impressed people."

Foxy waited for a reply but none came so he carried on with his thinking in a whisper.

"My parents never said, 'Hey, you're really good at that.' They used to just tell me how bad I was at things and my Dad used to shout at me all the time . . . like I was someone he'd found one morning in the kitchen he didn't know how to get rid of. Like he was confused what I was doing there in the first place."

A flash of light picked out the shapes in the hut as a match end flared up and died away. The red ember glow of a cigarette was all that remained, animating the flow of the words as it bobbed in sympathy with each syllable.

"People have a lot to answer for Al. Like Watson at school. He never did anyone any harm him you know. He was just born fat. He was born fat right, and he had to

155

wear glasses. And he didn't want to be born fat or anything and all that happened was that everyone had a go at him for looking different."

The cigarette end lit brightly and then dimmed again.

"So what happens is he starts getting to think that maybe he isn't as good as anyone else just 'cos he can't play football or something. See what I mean Al? And that takes years of ... that might take the rest of his life before he realizes that he's really quite a nice person. It's just all the other thick nasty people around him that made him think that ... People have a lot to answer for Al."

The ember glowed once more and was then extinguished. The rustle of Foxy's sleeping bag punctuated the silence as he turned over and found a comfortable position.

"I'm really quite a nice person Al ... Nobody ever told me that."

Alan's heavy breathing was the only reply.

"You know something Al? You're all right an' all ... For a moody git."

19

Foxy looked up from the slice of toast he was buttering as Alistair came back into the kitchen and spoke to him.

"I don't suppose you've got a better jacket than that have you boy?"

Foxy looked down at his brown leather jacket and frowned. He pulled at the sleeve as if looking for a mark on it then turned back to Alistair.

"What's wrong with this one?"

"Och, never mind. I'll get along to Stewart's, he'll lend you a jacket." Alistair bent to look at Foxy's trousers and then stood upright. "The trousers will need a brush but you'll do as you are."

Alistair then walked from the house and left Foxy staring questioningly at Alan, who was eating his toast silently.

"What was that about man? What's wrong with this jacket?"

"Nothing."

"Well what was all that about? What's he borrowing a jacket off Stewart for?"

"Alistair's taking us to church."

Foxy stared for a moment and then cocked his head on one side as if he was deaf.

"Eh?"

"I was going to tell you but I didn't get a chance."

"What chance. A chance for what?"

Alan sighed and cleared his throat.

"Well Alistair is a firm church goer. And if we want to keep on the right side of him and stay in the shed a few days more, then we've got to go along with it and go with him."

Foxy's brown eyes grew even bigger.

"I am bloody hellers like!"

"Foxy . . . it's only for . . ."

"Is this a joke or what!"

"Listen! Listen to me Foxy! We've got to. We have to if we want to stay here. I tried to get out of it last week but he wouldn't have it. It'll ruin everything if you refuse to go."

"That's a right stunt to pull on someone Al. Why didn't you tell me!"

"Because I knew this would happen that's why. Anyway, when was the last time you went to a church? It won't do any harm."

Foxy took a sip of his tea and banged the cup down.

"I've never been man. Ever. But I've seen it on TV and all they do is make you eat little biscuits and feel guilty."

Alan stood up.

"Well then it'll be a whole new experience for you won't it? Please Foxy. Don't make a mess of things. It's only an hour and then it's over."

"No! I'm not going man! I don't want to and I don't have to."

"Please Foxy. We'll have to leave if you don't go. It'll just cause so much bad feeling between us and Alistair that we'll have to go. You don't want to leave yet. Please Foxy. It's only an hour. You just sit down, stand up, sing a hymn and then go home again."

Foxy sat sullenly, staring at the pattern on the table cloth.

"I'm not going."

"Please Foxy. We've had a great time so far. It'll ruin . . ."

"I'm not bloody going!"

". . . It'll ruin everything if you don't go! Alistair's been really good to us. Not just me. He's been good to you Foxy. He's fed us and let us stay at his croft and we've just taken it from him. It won't cost anything to do this for him. Please Foxy."

Foxy said nothing. Then the outside door could be heard opening and Alistair strolled breezily into the kitchen. He held out the jacket to Foxy. It was quite plain but reasonably fashionable.

"There you go son. Almost made to measure."

Foxy looked at the jacket and narrowed his eyes. He stood up from the table and turned to Alistair.

"Yeah well," Foxy said and took the jacket. "Er . . . Yeah, well."

Foxy sat in the back of the car staring sullenly out of the window as they wove their way through the village and out past the croft. In the front seat Alan was fiddling with the tartan tie round his neck and Alistair was looking out at the sheep and crops.

"You're very quiet today boy. The rooster been getting you up too early again?"

Foxy glanced up and could see Alistair's eyes looking at him in the rear view mirror.

"Yeah," Foxy said quietly. "Didn't sleep very well."

When they reached the church Foxy followed a pace behind Alan as they entered the porch.

"I'm going to get you for this man."

"Oh shut up," Alan hissed back. "Do you think I'm enjoying it?"

"There might be something worth nicking anyway," Foxy whispered.

Alan turned round sharply and whispered at Foxy.

"You dare and I'll break your neck. I'm not kidding."

Foxy pulled a sneering face and followed as they moved forward into the interior of the dim church.

159

Alistair lead the way into the pew followed by Alan and then Foxy. Foxy stared with interest up and down the church as the rest of the congregation entered. He scratched his nose thoughtfully and turned to Alan.

"It's smaller than the one on tele."

"'Course it is, idiot. It's a village church, not a cathedral."

Foxy looked round the congregation, and suddenly pointed a finger at an old man on the other side of the aisle.

"A kilt!"

He said it so loudly that several people looked round. Alan elbowed him and hissed back.

"Shut up!"

"A kilt!" Foxy whispered. "He's got a kilt on."

"Good. You can die happy. Now shut up."

The minister came down the aisle and the congregation rose. Alan stood up quickly and hooked a hand under Foxy's arm so that he could pull him to his feet.

"Good morning," the minister said brightly. "Hymn two seven three."

Alan nudged Foxy and pointed to the red hymn book in front of them. They both picked one up and looked at the correct page. Neither of them knew the hymn.

The lady at the harmonium began treadling the pedals and the bellows wheezed noisily. She pedalled harder and harder until the wheezing noise almost sounded like a braying donkey and the chord filled the room.

Foxy's eyes went wider as he watched. By the time the singing started he was standing with his mouth wide open. Then he laughed and turned to Alan in astonishment.

Alan frowned and shook his head urgently to prevent Foxy from saying what ever it was that had suddenly sprung to mind. Foxy turned back to the hymn book and made a big show of miming to the song.

The hymn lost momentum at the second verse, in spite of the tremendous efforts of the lady at the back with the big hat. It faded at the third verse and by the fourth verse it was obvious even to Foxy and Alan that the hymn ended here.

The congregation sat down and shuffled as they tried to get comfortable on the hard wooden bench. Then the minister stepped up into the pulpit.

The minister stared round the congregation once, as if gathering in people's attention, then he leaned on the pulpit and suddenly thrust a pointed finger in the general direction of the middle pew.

Foxy looked nervously round and then sat lower in the seat as if trying to get the finger to aim over his head.

"Do you love your neighbour!" the minister said with such force that it was hard to tell whether it was a question or an accusation.

Foxy looked at Alan the same way he used to when caught doing something wrong in class.

"Chance would be a fine thing," he whispered.

Alan gave him a look and turned back to the front.

"The world is full of people," the minister said as he rocked back on his feet and settled into a more comfortable pose, "but do we love them? Do we really love them?

"No we don't!" the minister continued. "And do you know why? Do you know why?"

The minister waited to see if they knew why. They didn't know why.

"I'll tell you why," the minister said triumphantly. "I'll tell you why," the minister said again and stared hard at the speck on the front of the pulpit. He looked up at the congregation and smiled as if the speck on the pulpit had given him the answer. "Because we love ourselves too much."

Foxy flicked his eyes at Alan and then back to the

minister. As the sermon continued he felt he was missing something somewhere but he wasn't unduly worried. He put his hands in the pockets of Stewart's jacket. Mints. Half a packet of mints. He flipped one out with his thumb and popped it absently into his mouth.

"And now hymn three five two," the minister said as the congregation began to rise.

Foxy and Alan shuffled to their feet and opened the hymn book at hymn three five two. Foxy looked at it and then turned the hymn book upside down. It made little difference. He didn't know the hymn anyway.

Alan reddened with embarrassment as he felt Alistair staring disapprovingly at them.

20

"Are you trying to drown me or what!"

"Stop kicking your legs!"

"I've got to or I'll drown!"

Foxy stood up in the shallow water and coughed violently. His face was a red purple colour from the coldness of the water and the effort of learning to swim.

"That's it. Forget it man. I don't want to swim."

Alan waded nearer.

"That's not the right attitude. You said you wanted to try swimming this morning."

"Well that was this morning," Foxy said as he began to stride for the shore.

"Oh come on."

"No. I'm freezing."

"Just one more try Foxy. You nearly had it there."

"I nearly . . ." Foxy said as he coughed again and spat. "I nearly drowned! That's what I nearly did!"

Alan watched him walk to the shore and then followed him up the beach to the dip in the grass banks away from the wind. They both shivered in silence as they dressed, then Foxy found a flip of a cigarette in his jacket and lit it as he crouched in a huddle to smoke it.

"Man that was cold that was. I thought it was supposed to be summer."

"It is," Alan said as he pulled on his trousers and shirt. "We're not in the Mediterranean you know."

"You're telling me."

They sat on the grass and waited for their bodies to warm up. Foxy stubbed out the cigarette.

"You know something Al. This has been the best holiday I've ever had. Ever."

Alan smiled. "It's been great. I should have done this ages ago."

"Shame we have to go back."

"Yeah," Alan nodded, "but we can't stay here for ever. We've got to go back some time to face all that job stuff."

Foxy pulled up a wisp of spikey grass and began to wrap it slowly round his finger as he talked.

"I'm going to work with animals or something like that."

"What?"

"Yeah," Foxy said and pulled up another strand of grass. "I've thought about it. It'd be all right that."

"What? You?" Alan laughed. "You nearly ran a mile when we were dipping the sheep."

"I didn't know much about it then. Be fair man. That's the first time I'd ever been near the things. But anyway. I think it'd be good. Animals don't care who you are or anything. They don't give a damn about what you look like. Know what I mean?"

"Maybe."

"They only care about what you do to them. They don't care what you sound like or what you look like or anything. That seems great to me. Not having people judging you all the time." Foxy leaned back on his elbow as he stretched out his legs on the grass and looked across at Alan. "And I'm going to stop nicking things."

"What!"

"Well I'm going to try anyway."

"News at ten. Foxy today declared that he is going to stop nicking things."

"I'm serious man. It was like . . . getting faster and faster."

164

Alan looked at the expression on Foxy's face and realized that he was being serious.

"How do you mean?"

"I don't know, it's just . . ." Foxy squirmed uncomfortably. "When we were talking the other night . . . in the shed. I thought, I'm not really evil. Know what I mean? . . . I just take things. And then I started thinking about when our Terry used to take things off me when my Mum weren't watching. He used to steal my sweets and toys and stuff. It sounds daft, but I just remembered it that night . . . And it hurt that did . . . when he used to do that. It really hurt me . . . because I couldn't do anything about it.

"There was one time . . . it was building that fence that made me think of it. There was one time when I made a model. It was brilliant man. I made this model of a plane and I was right proud because I'd made it all by myself. I was only five or something and I was really proud because I'd made this model all by myself and I was waiting for my Mum to come back from the shops so's I could show it to her. And then our Terry grabbed it and stood on it. On purpose because he thought it was funny . . . And when she came back from the shops I was crying so much I couldn't explain what he'd done. I was crying that much that she just thought we'd been fighting or something. And I was just clutching this model. All broken up, and I was just clutching it and crying because our Terry had smashed it up."

Foxy sighed and moved his elbow to a more comfortable position.

"So I thought, that's what it must be like. When I steal things off someone. I don't know who they are so I can pretend that it doesn't really do any harm. But it would have hurt me just as much if Terry had smashed the model up while I was somewhere else . . . Because it was mine. So I felt a bit bad and decided that I'd stop nicking things. It was just getting faster and faster. Like . . . like it didn't really matter. It was all a laugh, but when you think about it it wasn't a laugh really. And if I get caught now I'm in big bother. It was O.K. when I was under sixteen, but not now."

Alan raised his eyebrows and looked at Foxy.

"I've learned a lot about you Foxy."

"Yeah?"

"Yeah. You're all right. You're a lot nicer person than you think you are."

Foxy grinned. "I know. I'm brill aren't I? So what about you then? What're you going to do?"

Alan shrugged. "I don't know exactly. But I've been having a think. I've thought about it a bit being out here away from it all and everything. Things look different from a distance somehow."

"Too true."

"And I've had a think about it. I thought . . . the only person who's holding me back from doing anything I want, is me."

"Yeah?"

"No listen. There's everybody going round blaming something else all the time. It's their parents' fault. Or it's the government's fault or bad luck or the weather or something. All the time they go round blaming something. And then I thought that maybe I could spend the rest of my life going round blaming something, or I could have a think about it and straighten it up a bit."

Foxy raised his eyebrows. "So what answer to the universe did you come up with then?"

Alan leaned back on the grass and crossed his legs out in front of him.

"It all stops somewhere. Listen, right. You start off by blaming your parents and then the teachers and then the government and then you run out of things. And when you come down to it they're all people. They're only people. So who told them what to do and who did they blame everything on all the time?"

Foxy frowned and put his hands behind his head.

"Beats me man."

"Exactly."

"Eh?"

Alan sat up and gathered his thoughts.

"The only person who can really do anything about me is me."

"Great."

"No. Listen. It's up to you. No-one else cares that much. They're too busy living their own lives . . . My life's my responsibility. No-one else's. Other people can help make things really bad or really good but they can't live your life for you. That's why I failed my exams. I thought someone would sort of wave a magic wand and all the stuff would be put in my head by a teacher or something. So when I failed I thought it was their fault."

Foxy laughed. "So being thick hadn't got anything to do with it then?"

Alan grinned and made to kick him.

"No. I mean, it was up to me that's all. That's what I've been thinking because of this holiday. It was me that decided to come up here and I just went and got on with it. If I'd waited for someone else to decide for me I'd still be waiting."

Foxy stood up and brushed the grass from his jeans.

"Yeah, well."He turned round as Alan stood up and began to follow him. "So are we really setting off tomorrow then?"

"Yeah?"

Foxy sighed. "Do you think we could come up next year?" He grinned and slapped Alan on the arm. "Hey, yeah! Why not eh? Can we come up next year? Alistair won't mind."

"Yeah, why not."

Foxy nodded happily and walked off through the grassy dunes.

"Yeah. We'll come up next year and help him chuck sheep about again. I liked that bit."

21

The clock on the mantelpiece seemed to tick louder than usual as Foxy and Alan waited. They were both sitting on the settee with their bags on the floor between their knees.

"Feels right sad doesn't it?" Foxy said as he shuffled on the settee and flipped the handles on his sports bag.

"Yeah," Alan said with an equally heavy voice.

Alistair came through from the kitchen and stopped as he saw the two forlorn figures crouched on his settee.

"My, my boys. It looks like death row." He smiled and sat in the old armchair by the fire.

"Soon be off now. What time did Stewart say?"

"Eight o'clock."

Alistair nodded and sighed slightly.

"Are you all right for money now boys? You don't want to be needing money on a long journey like that."

"No," Alan said. "We're fine. We've hardly spent anything since we've been here."

"Are you sure now? What about you Foxy?"

Foxy half smiled. "No. I'm O.K."

"Do you want another cup of tea before you go?"

They both shook their heads just as the car horn sounded outside the front door.

"That'll be Stewart now," Alistair said as he rose from the chair and went to the window. "Aye. He's here. You'd best be getting off then. It's a long journey, even with a lift to Inverness."

Foxy and Alan stood and waited uncomfortably as Alistair came back to them and extended his hand.

"Take care Foxy. Maybe you'll manage to get up here next year."

"Yeah. Ta, Alistair. It's been great. I've enjoyed it."

Foxy shook the outstretched hand and smiled unhappily as Alistair moved to Alan.

"And you boy. You'll send my regards to your parents and take care of yourself now?"

"Yeah. I'll be O.K. Thanks a lot Alistair."

"Och, nothing. I've enjoyed seeing you boys. You've been a good help to me."

"Well," said Alan as he shrugged. "Thanks anyway."

They both walked to the door, out into the brightly lit morning and walked in single file down the garden path, past the sheep dogs' sheds.

"Now then dogs? You working?" Foxy said as he tapped on the door with his fingers. There was a shuffling from inside and then two black noses could be seen pressing at the small gap in the wooden door. "See you then." The sound of a tail thumping against the woodwork followed them as they crossed the road to Stewart's car.

Alistair followed them to the gate and waited as they arranged themselves and their bags inside the car. Then as the car set off he raised his hand in a wave and watched them move down the main street of the village.

"Got everything?" Stewart asked as they coasted down the quiet street.

"Yes. I think so," Alan said and turned in the front seat to give one more wave to Alistair.

"What about you Foxy? Glad to be going back?"

"You must be kidding."

They drove through the village and out round the end houses. Occasionally they would pass one of the villagers walking along the road, who would stop and raise a hand at them. They both raised a hand in a return greeting.

When they passed the end of the croft Alan and Foxy

had their eyes glued to the fields. They saw the shearing pens disappearing behind them and the small shed they'd used as a chalet.

Foxy pointed at the fence in the field as they drove up to the top road.

"That's my fence man. I built that."

"We built that," Alan said from the front seat.

"Yeah," Foxy said. "But I knocked in all the posts. That'll be there for fifteen years that will."

They turned right at the top road and followed the same route to Dalstrath that they'd taken when riding the bikes.

"That's your ditch that is," Stewart said and pointed to the small drainage ditch down the side of the road.

Foxy laughed. "I nearly broke my leg man. That was a laugh that was. That black tank thing."

Foxy craned his neck to see through the hedge, down the fields to the distant sea and then settled back in the seat.

The car passed through the small town of Dalstrath and out towards the main road South. They fell silent as the fields and hedges passed them and they moved slowly further away from Tiener, back towards the South. Back to home.

When they eventually reached the far side of Inverness, Stewart pulled the car over and let them out.

"I can't take you any further," he said as he called through the open door at them. "But this'll give you a good start anyway."

Thanks," Alan said as he pulled his bag from the car and stood upright. "See you then. Might see you next year."

"Aye, maybe," Stewart nodded. "But I don't know where I'll be next year so we'll just have to see."

"Well good luck anyway."

"Thanks."

Foxy waited until Alan was looking down the road and

then dipped his head back into the car. He quickly put his hand in his pocket and slid something along the car seat to Stewart.

"I found this," Foxy said in a half whisper. "Can you take it back?"

Stewart looked at what Foxy had given him and nodded.

"Yeah, sure," he said, and put the red hymn book under the dash board. "I'll give it to Alistair."

Foxy smiled and stood up.

"See you then."

The old car grunted angrily as Stewart put it into gear and set off back up the road to Dalstrath. He raised a hand at them as he dipped his head in the mirror and then he was gone round the next bend in the road.

Foxy walked up to Alan and sighed.

"Well," he said as he looked down the road. "I suppose this is it."

"Yeah."

"Best get going then."

"Yeah."

"Best get ourselves off and go home."

"Yeah."

"Best get ourselves . . ."

"Shut up Foxy."

"Right."

22

Alan sat back down on the wooden bench and tapped his training shoes impatiently against the pavement as he looked at his watch. It was three o'clock and they'd arranged to meet in the pedestrian precinct about two. About two to Foxy, probably meant from two until four, Alan thought dryly.

The precinct was just as he'd left it. The same drab colours and buildings. There was even a lone crisp packet still blowing around in the breeze from the doorways of the department stores.

The graffiti on the back of the bench declared that Brownloaf was still a puff, even after Alan's two week absence. Nothing had changed.

He looked up as a tall young man came towards him through the other crowds of shoppers. He didn't recognize the face straight away, then realized that it was Pete. Riggy's friend.

"All right Alan."

"All right Pete. How you doing?"

Pete pulled a face and sat down on the bench.

"Not so good. Now then . . ." Pete said as he stuffed his hands in his pockets and sat forward. "Something really strange just happened."

"Yeah?"

"Yeah. I just saw Foxy."

Alan sat up. "Where? He's supposed to be meeting me here. Well he was supposed to be meeting me here about an hour ago."

"Yeah well," Pete said and half laughed. "I was passing

those flats he lives in and he was in the arms of two coppers."

"What?"

"Yeah," Pete continued. "They were putting him in a police car. Don't know what for. Mind that mate of his, Tony, he got done for something a couple of weeks ago. Broke into a Newsagents. Maybe it was something to do with that."

Alan leaned forward on the seat and sighed.

"Oh the daft . . ."

Pete was enjoying the fact that he had important news.

"Anyway, as I was passing, ol' Foxy shouted across to me. Across the road . . . He said he was meeting you here and to say he couldn't make it."

Alan nodded. "Not surprising is it with a copper on each arm."

Pete scratched his chin thoughtfully and looked directly at Alan. "And then he said to give you a message . . ." Pete looked blank for a moment as he tried to remember the exact words. "I don't know if this makes sense, right . . ."

"What?"

Pete cleared his throat. "Well . . . I don't know if this makes sense, right? This was just as they were putting him in the police car, right? But he said to give you this message . . . He said, 'Tell Red Wellies to bring some coconuts.'"

Alan stared for a moment and then sat back on the bench. He grinned and said nothing. Then he began to laugh. He laughed so loudly that people in the shopping precinct turned and stared.

Also in
Lions Tracks

To order direct from the publisher, just tick the titles you want and fill in the order form on the last page.

Lions Tracks